I WALK THE STREETS ALONE

A NOVEL by

THOMAS E. KRUPOWICZ

TERK BOOKS AND PUBLISHERS

Chicago, Illinois

Inside cartoon illustration drawn by **LEO FELTMAN**

Cover design by **STEVEN KRUPOWICZ**

ISBN # 1-881690-04-0

TERK BOOKS & PUBLISHERS
P.O. BOX 160
PALOS HEIGHTS, ILLINOIS 60463

This book is dedicated to my
two youngest grandchildren:

KYLIE (BOOMPA) KRUPOWICZ

&

STEPHEN (BUTCH) WINDY, JR.

Other books published by **TERK BOOKS & PUBLISHERS**

DEATH DANCED AT THE BOULEVARD BALLROOM
by Thomas E. Krupowicz
ISBN: 1-881690-00-8
12.95

FINGERPRINTS -- THE IDENTITY FACTORS
by Thomas E. Krupowicz
ISBN: 1-881690-01-6
39.95

FIRST LINE DEFENSE
by Thomas E. Krupowicz
ISBN: 1-881690-02-4
9.95

DEAD MEN DON'T DRINK VODKA
by Thomas E. Krupowicz
ISBN: 1-881690-03-2
14.95

**I've got to stop searching for more
of TERK's books!**

CHAPTER 1

A thunderous ovation, from the people occupying the seats in the Council Chamber of Chicago's City Hall, shook the walls causing sound waves to reverberate from the ceiling, forcing the main speaker to conclude his speech.

In the center of the Council Chamber, directly in front of the speaker's podium, fifty young candidates, both men and women, proudly held their certificates of achievement that officially announced their appointments to patrol officers.

Bright flashes from the press photographer's cameras illuminated the room as they recorded this special ceremony on film. This was a day that seemed so long in coming for these new police officers.

Vance Martall smiled as his eyes slowly surveyed the attending audience. He had a positive feeling of happiness in his heart. Although he was an orphan, he felt that someone in that large audience was cheering especially for him.

The heartbreaking tragedy of his past seemed so long ago. He remembered that horrible day he was placed in the custody of Provident Orphanage. An unforeseen disaster had left him without a family.

It was on the day of his ninth birthday. A flash flood had struck his community. His mother, father, little brother, and sister were swept away to a violent death in a surging, twisting river of muddy and murky water. Vance escaped a watery death by reaching the attic in his house and climbing out onto his roof.

As the rushing waters below him twisted and turned, desperately trying to destroy everything in its path, Vance escaped death by holding onto the roof shingles with every bit of strength that his frail young body could provide. As sunrise approached, help had finally arrived. Vance was transported to safety by helicopter.

The bodies of his family were never recovered. All efforts to locate any other living relatives had proved to be unsuccessful. Vance was finally placed in an orphanage by the Family Court.

1

Life at the orphanage was hard. The few worldly possessions that he called his own still had to be shared with the other children. He received very little for his own personal use.

His uncontrollable desire for reading and listening to music helped to sharpen his exceptional mind to absorb all the reading material that came within his grasp. Vance had a never ending thirst for knowledge and adventure. His lifetime desire was to become a law enforcement officer, but other duties and obligations came first.

On the day of his eighteenth birthday, Vance enlisted into the United States Army. The high scores that he produced on both his mental and practical tests demonstrated that his mind was as exceptionally fit as was his body. Viet Nam was his first stop after he completed his basic training.

Vance immediately blended in with his new comrades-in-arms. He became especially friendly with a bunk buddy named Paco Warez. Paco was an exceptional guitar player. He also had an extraordinary singing voice that blended in with the music that he played.

Vance had always wanted to play the guitar and create his own style of music. Paco finally gave in after three months of Vance's pleading and begging to teach him how to play the guitar. Each time they came in from searching the villages and jungles, looking for *Charlie*, Paco would spend some of his free time teaching Vance the basics of playing the guitar. It only took a short time for Vance to learn the letter sequence of the strings, as well as the basic chords that created the rhythmic music.

While the other soldiers went into a friendly village, looking for relaxation with women and booze, Vance continued on with his music education determined to accomplish his ultimate goal -- playing the guitar to the best of his ability.

On the thirteenth day of their eleventh month in Viet Nam, Paco Warez was shot in the chest during a fire fight just outside of a small jungle village. Paco laid on the ground for a few moments, stunned by what had happened to him. He tried to lift himself off of the ground, but the precious red life giving fluid that flowed out of his chest wound, made him weak.

Vance saw what had happened and crawled over to his friend. He applied a pressure bandage over Paco's chest wound, trying to stop the bleeding. The rifle fire became more intense. Paco knew that his time was near. He looked up at his friend. "It's no good, amigo. I'm gone. Get your ass out of here while you still can!"

Vance didn't say a word. He slung his rifle over his shoulder and began to lift his buddy off the ground. Paco grabbed hold of Vance's wrist with his blood soaked hand. "*I told you to get your ass out of here*," he screamed. Then he weakly said to Vance, "Promise me one thing, amigo." Paco paused to take a deep breath. "Take care of my guitar. Someday you'll master it. And when you do, then Paco will live on!" Paco Warez closed his eyes for the last time that day.

A half dozen more rifle shots rang out. Two bullets hit Paco's lifeless body. The other four bullets buried themselves into the ground next to Vance's right leg. The squad lost five men in the field that day.

Because of his ability and common sense reasoning, Vance was promoted to a special Army Intelligence Unit working both in the field and undercover with Black Market felons. Twice he was wounded and received battlefield commissions -- first to sergeant and then to lieutenant.

Visions of his past moved swiftly through his mind as Vance continued listening to the applause. At long last his most important boyhood dream had been achieved -- he was a police officer. He was confident that his knowledge and understanding of the law, along with his human behavioral science classes, would be beneficial in helping people who were in trouble and were dependent on him.

Vance smiled and let out a deep sigh of relief. He had finally made it. He was on his way -- at last.

The ceremonies drew to a conclusion. The applause ended. The audience stood up and began to leave. The new police officers congratulated each other as their relatives snapped photographs for the family photo albums.

Vance started to leave the Council Chamber when he felt a strong hand grasp his shoulder.

"Officer Martall, will you please come with me. I have some special instructions for you," said a tall, heavily built man wearing sergeant stripes on his white shirt sleeves.

"Yes sir, Sergeant Shaw," replied Vance. He followed the sergeant out of the Council Chamber, down a long corridor into a drab painted room. The sergeant walked behind a desk, sat down, opened the middle drawer and removed a brown manila envelope. Vance remained standing.

"Vance, as long as we're alone, lets skip the formalities and just call each other by our first name."

"That fine with me, Jim," replied Vance.

"I don't know what you've done or what this is actually all about, but I have some special orders here for you."

"Special orders for me? What kind of orders? I'm supposed to report to the Thirty-Third District Station tonight, working a patrol beat car on the midnight watch," remarked Vance, disturbed by Sergeant Shaw's last statement.

"As of this moment," interrupted the sergeant, "those orders are canceled. Now listen to what I tell you -- and listen carefully. This conversation ends in the confines of this room. You're not to repeat anything we talk about here -- not to anyone! Once you leave here, that's it -- understand?" Sergeant Shaw's voice had a dead serious tone.

"Yes Jim, I understand. Please go on."

"As far as any of your friends are concerned, you're assigned to the Thirty-Third District Station house, but you had to take an emergency medical leave. Tomorrow morning at exactly 0800 hours you're to report to room 105 here in City Hall. You'll wear civilian clothes. Have your badge, hat shield, identification card, service and off-duty revolvers with you."

"Can't you give me some kind of a clue on what's going on, Jim?" Vance pleaded.

"That's all I can tell you Vance. Actually, I don't know any more about this than what I've just told you." Sergeant Shaw stood up and shook hands with the new rookie. He smiled, remarking, "Good luck kid."

Vance stared at the sergeant for a long moment, then smiled. "I'll probably need it Sarge." Vance turned and left the office. He didn't realize then, how true and apropos his parting words would be.

CHAPTER 2

Vance had an uneasy feeling that today was a day that would bring a turning point in his life. Why? He wasn't yet quite sure. It was just a strange feeling that he had deep down in his gut.

Breakfast tasted good, but Vance had trouble keeping it all down. The butterflies he felt in his stomach were fluttering in all directions. Glancing at his wrist watch, he walked through the large glass entrance doors of City Hall at exactly 7:55 a.m.

Extremely nervous, Vance slowly approached a dark painted wooden door displaying white painted numbers, 105, trimmed with gold paint. His knock on the door was loud enough to be heard, but not loud enough to sound very demanding. A voice from within the office replied, "*Come in!*" Vance turned the door knob slowly, opened the door and walked into the office, closing the door behind him. A distinguished looking man sat behind a large oak desk. Rays of sunlight danced brightly through the window, resting softly on his salt and pepper colored hair. A neatly trimmed mustache rested on his lip above a friendly smile. The crow's feet lines at the corners of his eyes and deep lines about his mouth made Vance guess that the man's age was around sixty-two.

"Can I help you young man?" The man asked courteously.

"Yes sir, you can. I'm Officer Vance Martall. I was instructed to report here this morning at exactly 8:00 a.m."

"Sit down, Officer Martall," said the stranger, stroking his chin lightly with the tips of his fingers. "Please excuse me a moment." He lifted the receiver off of the telephone cradle, dialed a number and waited for someone to answer at the other end of the line. "It's me sir," he finally said into the mouthpiece, "Captain Reese." He paused. "Yes, he's here now." Instructions were given to him from the other end of the phone line. The man placed the receiver back on the telephone cradle, got up from his chair and walked over to the window. He looked out the window without saying anything else to Vance.

Captain Reese, thought Vance. Where did I make a mistake big enough to have one of the big brass asking to see me?

The passing minutes seemed like hours. Suddenly, the office door flew open. Two men entered the office. Vance looked up at them, trying to force a friendly smile.

"Officer Martall, I'm Mayor Cotagney," said the shorter of the two men. "And this is Police Commissioner Linton who I'm sure you already recognize. The gentleman standing at the window is Captain Reese of our Special Field Task Force Unit."

Vance jumped up from his chair and stood at attention, just as he had been taught to do at the police academy when he met one of the big brass. Mayor Cotagney smiled. "Sit down Officer Martall and relax. You're not here for a disciplinary or board of inquiry hearing." Vance was glad to take advantage of the mayor's offer.

Mayor Cotagney walked behind the desk and sat down. The commissioner made himself comfortable in a chair next to the mayor's desk. Captain Reese, carrying a brown folder, walked over to the desk and placed it in front of the mayor. Mayor Cotagney opened the folder and briefly read its' contents before looking up at Vance.

"I'm sure you're wondering what this is all about Officer Martall."

"Yes Mister Mayor, I am," Vance replied anxiously.

The mayor continued. "Before I give you an explanation, I'd like a few answers to some simple questions. First of all, you are twenty-one years old?"

"Yes sir, I was twenty-one on the sixteenth of April."

"You're five feet eleven inches tall, weigh one hundred and sixty-five pounds, have blue eyes, and brown hair?"

"Yes sir to all of your questions," replied Vance, wondering where all of this was leading.

"You served in the Armed Forces and did some undercover work for Army Intelligence. Is this all true?"

"Yes sir, I did," replied Vance again.

"One last question, Officer Martall. Is it true that you don't have any living relatives?" The mayor looked straight into Vance's eyes.

"That's right, sir. My family died when I was nine years old. I've been an orphan ever since then."

Mayor Cotagney closed the folder and spoke firmly. "Officer Martall, we have a special assignment that is of the utmost importance to us and this fine city. We've decided that *you are* the best man for this assignment."

"Special assignment? Me sir? What kind of assignment?" asked Vance -- eager and yet puzzled.

"I'm sure you're aware of the fact that within the last year, crime has risen among the teen-age population of this city. Many people have asked the question, why? The answer to that question, Officer Martall, is narcotics. Narcotics has torn down the morals and the ambitions of today's American youth. The teenagers of today don't want a career, position, family, respectability, recognition, or wealth. All they want to do is destroy themselves with the help of drugs or whatever other means they can find. Their other goal is the destruction of this establishment -- that's us!

"Don't get me wrong, Officer Martall, not all of America's youth is infected with this dirty disease. Only a very small minority, but every day their numbers increase and soon that minority will be the majority. Most of these kids are hooked on drugs. They have to steal and commit other crimes to get the necessary money to pay for their drug habits. We've got to do something about this problem, and this is where you come into the picture. We need a man to go undercover -- out in those streets. We need someone who's young. He can't have family ties who could blow his cover on the street if they recognized him. Officer Martall, the street out there is virtually a jungle -- a drug jungle -- *a spiked jungle!* It's as though drugs, such as heroin and crack cocaine along with hypodermic needles, are on bushes just growing wild out there in the streets.

"We need vital information on the activities of active addicts, pushers and suppliers. You'll take this assignment on a voluntary basis, of course, and you'll walk the streets -- all alone. You'll be completely isolated from the normal way of living. You'll carry no identification that will identify you as a police officer. You'll have to turn in your badge, hat shield, identity card and firearms. Your police uniforms and good civilian clothes will be placed into storage. You'll have to find a new place to live. Your paycheck will be placed into a special account each payday. You can withdraw your money when you've completed your assignment. You'll have to get a job and supply your own lively hood while out on the streets. Well Officer Martall, that's the whole story in a nut shell. What's your answer? Will you take the assignment?"

Vance squirmed uneasily in his chair. He felt as though he had been pushed into a corner with no way to escape. "Your Honor, it's a rough decision to make. I've worked so hard and waited so long to become a uniformed officer," pleaded Vance.

"It's an important assignment," interrupted the mayor. "Your decision has to be made *here* and *now!*"

Vance reacted quickly. That was something his time in Viet Nam had taught him. "All right sir," he paused, "I'm your man. I'll take the assignment."

Vance stood up and placed his police equipment on top of the desk. At the conclusion of shaking hands with the three men, Vance started to leave, but suddenly stopped. Turning around he asked, "What's my code name in this new unit?"

The Mayor's eye caught the numbers on the open door. "The unit's numbers will be 105 and your code name will be -- *TEDDY BEAR.* You'll use that name as an alias if you're ever arrested by the police. Captain Reese will review all of the previous days arrest reports. If he runs across that name, he'll check to see if it's you in the lock-up. When you have to get in touch with any of us, put your information in an envelope, address the initials *T.B.* and send the envelope to City Hall in care of this room. We'll handle things from this end. Captain Reese will also give you his special home telephone number, but that number is to be used only in a matter of life or death."

Vance nodded his head, gesturing that he understood everything that he was told, and then left the office. He walked a few feet, turned and looked back at the closed door. Scratching his head, he thought, *TEDDY BEAR*? Oh well, looks like I'm a civilian again.

Walking through the exit door of City Hall, Vance braced himself for his new and totally unexpected career. He wondered if he really had it in him to see it through successfully.

CHAPTER 3

Everything proceeded according to the Mayor Cotagney's plan. The construction of Vance's new identity was left entirely up to him. The weeks that followed were spent entirely in preparation for it. His clothes were collected and placed in storage. Leaving his comfortable apartment, he maintained a room in the run down section of the city. He stopped shaving and having his hair cut. He kept only enough money to get by on. Canned beans, hamburgers, hot dogs, and cold lunch meat became his steady daily diet. Vance also neglected the use of a bathtub. After all, if he wanted to be accepted by these special people, he had to blend in with the odor.

Vance's biggest problem was to find an odd hobby or occupation -- something to relieve his so-called frustrations and tensions. Too many poets, painters and philosophers were already roaming the streets looking for individuals to recognize their crafts.

Vance's knowledge of the guitar would be of great help to him. He also selected photography as a money earning profession. Oh, he wasn't the regular everyday type of photographer. Vance decided to be a pop art photographer. Taking pictures through broken pieces of colored glass would be his special trait. He could develop his own photographs. He planned on showing them off to everyone that he met and rave about how wonderful they looked. He'd explain to people that his photographs illustrated an addict's view of the world as it looked to him when he took his trip to infinity and back again to the real world. His plan should help him get accepted into the jungle community. Only a true nut would make this profession his life's ambition.

Maybe the curiosity seekers of the misfit set wouldn't accept his guitar playing, but he was positive that the regulars and addicts would like his photography. Anyway, the time was right and Vance was ready. Now he'd start to earn his salary.

The rays from the early morning sunlight found their way through the broken window panes, resting gently on Vance's face. He slowly rolled over and got up off of a sagging mattress that represented his bed. Vance walked over to the window and looked down at the street below. His eyes focused on the pawn shop window directly across the street from his room.

In the window, a large old-fashioned clock rested on a chipped section of shelving. The hands displayed the time -- 8:30 a.m. Vance turned away from the window and walked over to a patched drum table in one corner of the room. He removed two slices of hard bread and a shriveled up hot dog from a plastic bag. He spread some mustard on one slice of bread, sliced up the hot dog and buried it in the mustard. He opened his mouth and ate. This was his breakfast.

Turning, he walked towards the doorway. He stopped and looked into a broken piece of mirror hanging on the wall. For a long while he just stared at an ugly image that started back at him. In total disgust, he mumbled aloud, *"Oh brother!"* He picked up his guitar, slung it over his shoulder, then left the room. Walking slowly, he stopped to admire the beautifully decorated hallway. Only a few more little touches were needed to make it really perfect -- some plaster to seal up the holes in the ceiling and walls and some shades over the light bulbs.

Vance walked along the hallway, down the broken stairwell and out into the street. Reaching into his pocket, he counted the entire contents -- thirty-three dollars.

Better get a camera and developing kit first, he thought, shoving the money back into his pocket. He walked over to the pawn shop and went inside. The proprietor was a short man with a belly that hung an inch over his pant's belt. He chewed vigorously on an old cigar stub that looked as though he'd been gnawing on it for a week.

"Got something to sell kid?" he asked, looking at Vance's guitar. "If that's hot, I don't want it!"

"No," replied Vance. "I ain't got nothin' to sell. I wanna buy a camera, that's if you got a good one for the right price."

"*You wanna buy something,*" shouted the pawn shop owner. "Say, that's a switch. Usually you junkies are sellin' somethin'."

Vance felt his blood start to boil. Being called a junkie was not exactly to his liking. "*Whadoya mean by calling me a junkie,*" he screamed at the top of his voice.

"Oh, I'm sorry I hurt your delicate feelings," remarked the pawn shop owner, laughing at Vance. "Let me rephrase that. I mean hippie not junkie."

"O.K. pal, now that you've had your morning chuckle, how about that camera I came in here for?" said Vance, calming down.

"How much do you want to spend kid?"

Vance reached into his pocket and placed two crumpled ten dollar bills on the counter. "Twenty bucks," he replied proudly.

The pawn shop owner removed a camera from the top shelf directly behind him and tossed it to Vance. "How about that beauty. Like it?"

"Come on, what're you tryin' ta pull," sneered Vance. "This is nothin' but a plain box camera. You can buy these for a *fin* in any drug store. I wanna camera that I can change the focus and shutter speed."

"You know what you're talkin' about, don't you kid?" remarked the pawn shop owner, changing his tone of voice.

"Yea, I know somethin' about cameras."

The stout man disappeared into the back room and came back carrying another camera. "If you can come up with another five, I'll sell you this camera for twenty-five."

Vance took the camera and looked it over carefully. With his knowledge of cameras, he knew that this camera was expensive and sold for well over two hundred dollars. That meant it had to be stolen. He placed the camera back on the counter.

"Forget it, pal. I told you I only had twenty bucks to spend. Besides, that camera must really be hot if you only want twenty-five for it." Vance turned and started for the door.

"Hold it kid. Wait just a moment. Gimme the double saw buck and the camera is yours."

Vance hesitated for a moment, just looking at the shop owner. Finally, he bought the camera and left the pawn shop. On the way back to his room, he thought, things were really happening for him. He now knew of a good fence to dump some hot merchandise if ever he had to convince anyone that he really was a street bum. In the meantime, he continued thinking, I'll have to tip the Captain about the pawn shop and have his men keep it under surveillance. I've gotten a hot camera now and if ever I'm caught with it, it'll give me a good cover story. Yea, things are starting to come together already, but I've got to watch that temper of mine. I can't fly off the handle every time someone makes fun of me or calls me names. All I've got to do is to make sure that people think, *I am,* what they want me to be...

CHAPTER 4

Vance was now ready for some real action. Before the morning had passed, he was ready to make use of his new identity. He slung his guitar over his shoulder, so it rested on his back, and hung the camera around his neck with a piece of common rope. Looking shabby and blending in with the surroundings was most important.

The bells in the church tower several blocks away chimed 6:00 p.m. Vance felt a hollow, hungry feeling inside of his stomach. It was that time again, the time that only the elite called dinner.

Vance left his room. Examining his neighborhood surroundings was next on his agenda. He'd also search for a classy hamburger joint to fill his empty stomach. The night air was warm and felt inviting as it gently brushed his sweaty brow.

Vance strolled along Carlton street. He viewed the hippie set sitting on the sidewalks and on stairways in most of the buildings that he passed. Several people strummed on guitars while others recited their home-brew poetry. The stench coming from the garbage cluttered alley was overwhelming. Vance suddenly lost his appetite for food. Instead of eating, he stopped to talk with a young couple sitting in one of the empty store doorways. Vance introduced himself, saying that he had just come into town. The young couple invited him to sit down and *rap* with them. Vance inquired about hot spots to go for kicks and where most of the teenagers made the scene for a good time.

Their conversation was cut short by the shrilling wail of a police siren. A tall, thin figure darted out from the dark shadows of a corner building across the street from them. The person headed straight for Vance. His blond hair was shoulder length. He wore a black and yellow striped tee-shirt, dark brown moccasins, and bleached stone beaten denim pants. Around his neck, on a silver chain, hung a .50-caliber machine gun bullet that reflected short bursts of light, from the bright street lights directly above him, as he passed them.

He grabbed hold of Vance's arm. The young man, appearing to be in his late twenties, was breathing heavily. His hand shook unsteadily. "Help me, will ya," he pleaded. "The cops are after me. I need a place to hide." The stranger clutched a clock radio under his right arm pit.

Vance gave the stranger a quick once over look. This was his opportunity to get in good with someone from this neighborhood. If he helped this character out, it might help him get into a local gang.

The flashing blue and white lights, on top of the police cars, caught Vance's attention as they passed the intersection two blocks away. He had to think fast. Jumping up, he grabbed the seedy looking stranger by his arm and pulled him in the direction of a dark alley. They were half way down the alley when a police car screeched to a stop. A deep, harsh voice from the direction of the police car shouted, "*Halt! Stop or we'll shoot!*"

Vance and the stranger kept on running. Two loud cracks of gun fire echoed through the alley. Vance could hear the scream of the lead pellets as they flew by his ear. Both men ran through the back door of a tenement building, slamming the door shut behind them. They propped it shut using a handy chunk of wood. Vance and his new found friend quickly made their way up to the roof top of the building. The tall stranger still clung on tightly to the clock radio.

"*Give me that damn radio,*" shouted Vance.

"What the hell you talkin' about man?" replied the stranger. "I went through a lot of trouble to get this radio. I need some bread for a fix. I'm not gonna give it up now."

"Listen to me stupid. I'm only tryin' to help you," said Vance. "Can't you get that through your thick fuckin' skull? I'm in deep shit now, just as much as you are. We're gonna have to jump across these roof tops. When we get back down to that street, we can't afford to be caught carrying this thing. We've got to get rid of it -- *NOW!* If we're caught, it's the cop's word against ours and they can't pin anything on us if they don't catch us with any loot."

Vance yanked the radio from under the stranger's arm and threw it down a chimney shaft next to them. The young stranger's face turned chalk white as he watched Vance drop the radio down the shaft. It looked as though he was going to jump down the shaft after the radio.

"*Are you nuts?*" screamed the stranger, grabbing the front of Vance's shirt. "*I'll kill you for what you just did -- mother fucker,*" he shouted angrily.

"We'll talk about that later." Vance pulled away from the stranger's grasp. "But first, let's get the hell away from here -- *NOW!*"

Vance held onto his guitar and camera as they jumped across roof separations and over roof partitions, successfully making their way down to the street below. Vance's knowledge of police emergency procedures helped him and his new companion to elude the police officers and flee the area.

Running for as long as their breath held out, they finally stopped to rest in front of a small, run-down restaurant. Vance looked at the tall stranger and offered him an understanding smile.

"Are you hungry?" he asked.

"I'm not hungry, man, but I could sure use a cup of hot and sweet coffee."

"Let's go in. It's my treat," said Vance. "I'll pop tonight. By the way, what's your name?"

"Stripes!"

"Stripes? Stripes what?" asked Vance.

"It's just plain old Stripes. I like striped threads. That's all I ever wear. Everyone calls me Stripes because of my clothes. I just got stuck with that name."

"Don't you ever use a last name?" asked Vance, being curious.

"Nobody around here uses a last name," replied Stripes. "By the way, what're you called?"

"Va-------!" Vance caught himself before revealing his real name. Another trap that he had to watch out for. "I've been known by a lot of different names in the past. Why not just pick one out that you like for me?"

They entered the small restaurant and sat in a booth next to the large plate glass window. Vance placed his guitar on the seat next to him. "I like to watch people and see what is going on." He explained. "That's why we sat here next to the window."

"What'll you guys have?" barked the owner from behind the counter.

"Two hot cups of coffee and a couple of dogs with everything on them," said Vance.

"Say, is that a working camera you've got hanging around your neck?" asked Stripes.

"Yea." Vance laughed. "I take this camera and my guitar wherever I go. They're both with me all of the time. I sing and play the guitar and also take pop art pictures through colored pieces of broken glass with this camera. Those crazy type distortions get me some wild pictures that I can sell to make some bread."

"Hey," laughed Stripes, "I got just the right name to fit you. Since a camera makes a clicking sound when you press the shutter button, I'll call you -- Clicker!"

"If that's the name you like, Stripes, then Clicker it is," laughed Vance.

"I want to thank you for helping me out, Clicker. I'd never have gotten away from those cops without your help."

"Forget it, Stripes. What's a pal for if you can't count on him when you're in a pinch?"

The restaurant owner brought their order over to the booth, setting everything down on the table, along with the bill. Vance dropped the exact amount of change on top of the bill after he read it. The owner scooped the money into the palm of his hand, counted it, and walked away mumbling to himself.

"Say, Stripes," said Vance, trying to speak with a mouth full of food, "is that a live bullet hanging on that chain around your neck?"

"Yes and no," said Stripes displaying a weird smile. "The primer on this shell is alive. I took some of the powder out of the casing. That's where I keep my drugs, man."

"You keep drugs in there? Are you a pusher Stripes?" Vance tried to act surprised.

"Sure, that's how I make money for my own habit. I sell drugs and steal whatever I can rip off. I pack the drugs in a plastic bag and place it next to the primer. I keep just enough black powder in the casing to cover the plastic bag. Then I push the metal pellet back into the front of the casing. If someone gets nosy and opens the front of the shell, all they'll see is the black powder."

"Did you figure that little gimmick out by yourself?"

"Sure, pretty clever, huh?" Stripes slowly sipped the hot coffee and took a bite of his hot dog. His mood suddenly changed. "Hey Clicker, how about showing me some of your pictures?"

Vance had to think fast. He didn't have any pictures on hand to show to Stripes. He had to come up with some kind of explanation. "I haven't any shots with me right now Stripes."

"Why not?" asked Stripes, displaying a tone of suspicion in his voice.

"I quickly left my last pad by way of the back window. We were having a pot party, when the cops came and busted down the front door. The only things I got away with was my guitar and the clothes on my back. I bought this camera this morning from a hock shop across from where I'm living. Tell you what Stripes, how about going out with me tomorrow? We'll take some pictures and I'll show you how it's done."

"Sounds good to me, Clicker."

Finishing their dogs and coffee, they left the restaurant. Walking along together for several blocks, they talked about Stripes' connections and the *in* places where they could get a few kicks.

"Where do you live Stripes? I'll meet you there in the morning," asked Vance, sounding a little bit too eager to end the night's festivities.

"Right now Clicker, I'm living anywhere I can find a place to park my ass: parks, doorways, the back seats of abandoned cars. Makes no difference to me."

"You don't have a regular place where you stay?" Vance was surprised.

"No," Stripes continued, "seems like I can't hold onto money long enough to pay for a place to live."

15

Vance changed his motivation. "I've got an idea, Stripes. I live alone. Why not double up with me at my place? The room is big enough for the both of us to live in. If we pool our bread together, it'll be easier to eat and pay the rent. At least you'll have a roof over your head and a regular place to come home to when it rains. It'll keep your ass dry."

"I don't know, Clicker." Stripes scratched the top of his head with his fingers. "I've been a loner for so long, I don't think I could get used to living with another person."

"Come on," laughed Vance, giving a small tug on his new friend's arm, trying to lead him in the direction of his skid-row hotel. "Why not try it for a few days and see how things work out? If you don't like it, you can pack up and leave. There's no chains that'll hold you there. It's no jail."

"It might not be such a bad idea," said Stripes, hesitating for a brief moment. "Where do you live?"

"How about coming home with me now? I'm only a few blocks from here."

"No," Stripes snapped back nervously, "I've got a few loose ends that I have to tie up tonight. Got some people to meet."

"Want me to tag along with you?" Vance tried to conceal just how anxious he really was to go with his new friend.

"No," Stripes hesitated, " you'd better not. Not tonight anyway. Just give me your address and I'll meet you at your place in the morning."

Vance shrugged his shoulders, then said, "Twenty-five Kelter Street. It's the *STOP AND FLOP* Hotel. Go up the staircase to the second floor and turn to your right. It's room 2A at the far end of the hall."

They both smiled as they shook hands. Vance walked slowly in the direction of his hotel. Stripes turned and quickly walked off in the opposite direction to meet with his mysterious people. Vance would have given anything to have stayed with Stripes, but he knew he just had to be a little patient. His time would come soon enough...

CHAPTER 5

Loud pounding on the wooden door woke Vance from a troubled dream. He opened his eyes, slowly surveying the dismal room. He tried to analyze if he was awake or still dreaming. He shut his eyes, rolled over and started drifting back into a deep sleep. The loud pounding persisted.

"*Who is it?*" he shouted angrily.

"It's me man, me," came the reply from behind the closed door.

"*Who in the hell is me?*" shouted Vance.

"Stripes, man. Did you forget about me already?"

"Oh, Stripes! Just a second." Vance leaped off the bed, pulled up his pants, walked over to the door and flung it open. "I'm sorry. I was asleep. I didn't realize it was you knocking. Come on in and make yourself comfortable."

Stripes walked into the room strutting like a proud peacock displaying a fine array of colorful new feathers. He gave the room a quick once over, then walked over to the makeshift bed and sat down.

"Say, this place is O.K."

"It's home," answered Vance. "You're really riding high today Stripes? Can I ask why?"

"I negotiated a great deal last night and I'm rollin' in dough today Clicker." Stripes reached into his right front pant's pocket and pulled out a thick roll of bills held together with a rubber band that could choke a horse. "How much dough will you need for rent and food, Clicker?" he asked.

"Fifty bucks should cover it." Vance was flabbergasted at the sight of all that money. "But," he hesitated, "where did you get all that dough?"

"Never mind." Stripes changed the topic of the conversation. "Let's go out. I want to see just how you take those crazy pictures."

"Sure, but first I've got to get a developing kit and some film."

"No problem, pal, no problem." Stripes counted off ten pieces of green paper from the top of the stack and handed them to Vance. Vance tucked the money into his pocket and picked up his camera and guitar.

They left the hotel in search of a camera shop where they could get the supplies that Vance needed.

The entire afternoon was spent photographing scenery, objects and people in unusual settings and positions. Stripes selected what he wanted photographed, and Vance took the pictures. Using different gimmicks, Vance shot some very interesting photographs. Sprinkling drops of water on the lens of the camera would produce a picture that had perfect focus, but disfigurement of both people and objects. Covering the camera lens with different thickness' and colors of broken pieces of glass also gave his pictures varied assortments of different illusions. After many hours of wandering, they returned to their hotel room to develop the rolls of film.

Stripes laid down on top of the bed and rested the back of his head on his hands. "Man, my dogs are really barking," he groaned, kicking his shoes off.

Vance cleaned off the counter top and wiped the scum from inside the sink. Turning on the cold water, he let it run freely. Removing a few plastic containers off the cabinet shelf, he placed them on top of the counter. He carefully removed two bottles of liquid developer from a carton, uncapped both bottles and poured some of the liquid from each bottle into separate trays. Unscrewing a light bulb from the socket of a low hanging ceiling fixture, Vance replaced the original bulb with a colored bulb, specifically designed for developing negative and positive prints. He turned on the colored light and started the slow developing process. The film was dipped into different solutions producing negatives that could reproduce pictures. Vance used the negatives to print photos on positive paper. When he was finished, he hung the photographs up to dry.

Vance looked at Stripes. He was laying on the bed, now sound asleep. Stripes tossed and turned restlessly, mumbling phrases that meant nothing to Vance.

Suddenly, Stripes sat straight up and let out a loud, terrifying scream. Stunned by the sudden outburst, Vance nearly fell backwards off the chair his ass was perched on. Beads of perspiration dropped from Stripes' forehead. He sat up shivering in the center of the bed.

"What the hell is wrong with you?" asked Vance, deeply concerned.

"I'll be all right in a little while. Don't worry about it! Better get used to it if I'm gonna be livin' here with you. I get these little attacks every once in a while. The doctors have referred to it as kind of a withdrawal symptom. It's been a while since a had my last fix. Once I turn on, I'll be fine. Where's the John?"

"It's the center door at the far end of the hall," replied Vance, pointing in the direction.

"I'll be back in a couple of minutes." Stripes was obviously in pain. He crawled out of bed and tried to stand up straight. His body continued to shake as beads of perspiration appeared on his forehead. He looked at Vance and tried to smile. Suddenly, he doubled up, grabbing his stomach with both hands, screaming from the pain. His facial features changed completely. Stripes fought to keep from vomiting in the room. Turning around quickly, he ran through the doorway, down the hallway, into the bathroom.

Vance could hear Stripes gagging. After several minutes there was nothing but silence. Vance decided that he'd better investigate.

The bathroom door was partially open. Vance pushed it open the rest of the way to completely see inside of the room. Stripes was sitting on the floor, huddled in the far corner of the room. A filthy tarnished spoon, its handle curved inwards, laid on the floor next to him. In the cup of the spoon rested a small charcoal colored wad of cotton. Several burnt matches laid next to the spoon. Stripes had rolled the pants covering on his right leg up over his knee cap. A piece of rubber tubing was tied securely around his thigh so the veins and arteries in his leg would swell.

Stripes had just finished injecting a grayish colored liquid into the back of his knee, with the help of a dirty hypodermic needle. He pulled the needle out from the skin, closed his eyes and rested his head against the stained wall. A look of relief and contentment soon dominated his facial expression. He opened his eyes slowly, only to be startled by the sight of Vance watching him from the opened doorway.

"You're a mainliner," said Vance, not really surprised. "I thought that you said you only smoked pot?"

Stripes stared blankly at Vance and remained silent. The long, thin, black track marks on his leg drew Vance's attention.

That hypo needle has done its' job well, thought Vance. It's permanently labeled him for the rest of his life.

19

Stripes untied the rubber tubing around his thigh and slowly lifted himself off the floor. He slid up the corner of the wall to keep from falling.

"Well, are you gonna close the door and let me take a piss or are you gonna just stand there and admire my dick?" Stripes remarked jokingly.

Vance felt disgusted, but realized that he couldn't show any signs of emotion. "I'll see you back in the room." He turned and gave a short wave.

Minutes later, Stripes came strolling back into the room -- smiling. All the signs of his unbearable agony had disappeared. "Have you finished developing all the negatives yet?"

"Sure, only it's gonna take a couple of hours for them to dry. We'll have to let them hang on this line." Vance lifted the window shade and looked down at the street below. The hands on the clock in the pawn shop window showed 8:15 p.m. The sun had set and the sky was filled with twinkling stars.

"Well, as long as we can't do anything else around here, let's go out for a walk," suggested Stripes. Vance agreed. They started their stroll down Tate Street. Curiosity seekers crowded the sidewalks. They were the usual Saturday night tourists, anxious to see how the so-called weirdo's lived.

Artists, hopeful of making a living, displayed their paintings on the sidewalks and fences. Girls of every age and size also displayed their wears, occasionally stopping a man or two who looked like they might be a good prospect. The flashing multi-colored neon lights above the many store windows lit up the street with the illusion of festivity.

Several people stopped to talk with Stripes and Vance, while others just waved and passed them by. It was apparent to Vance that Stripes was very popular with the people from this section of town. A guy didn't have to be a genius to figure out why. Vance had discovered that answer back in the hotel bathroom.

As they took their leisurely walk, occasionally stopping to look at the displays in the store windows, they were suddenly approached by a young man and girl walking from the opposite direction. The man, in his early twenties, was dressed in skintight buckskin clothes. His light brown hair hung shoulder length. Covering his lip and chin was a full mustache and Van Dyke beard.

The girl was in her late teens. Vance eyed her body with a quick throb of desire. Her unusual walk resembled a graceful deer prancing slowly through a forest in the early morning hours. There was a crisp freshness about her when she smiled. The dark, tight fitting denim jeans she wore revealed every curvaceous line of her torso. The fringe on her buckskin jacket swayed rhythmically as she walked. Her black straight hair, hanging well below her shoulders, revealed a twinkling luster beneath the flashing multi-colored neon lights. A brightly colored Apache headband caressed her forehead tightly. Vance just couldn't take his eyes off of her.

"Hi Stripes! Ain't seen you all day. Where you been?" inquired the young man.

"Been settling down in my new pad. I'm living over on Kelter Street now. Oh, by the way, this is my new roomie. Clicker, this is Sorento and the pretty girl is Monica." The girl smiled at Vance, displaying her pearl white teeth. Sorento started to speak, but suddenly froze. He shot his friend a harsh glance and motioned for Stripes to follow him.

While Stripes and Sorento talked, Monica and Vance did too. Vance managed to keep Sorento and Stripes in full eye's view. Monica spoke with a soft pleasing tone, being cautious to choose the right words to say. She was careful not to reveal too much information about herself.

At the corner of his eye, Vance saw Stripes slip a small packet to Sorento. Sorento quickly tucked the packet into his pocket. Vance knew that it was a delivery. He had to act uninterested about what was going on before him. It was important that he give the impression that his only interest at that moment was Monica.

After several more minutes of conversation, Stripes and Sorento rejoined Vance and Monica. With one sweeping motion, Sorento grabbed Monica's arm and walked passed Vance without saying a single word to him. Monica turned, smiled, and gave Vance a short wave as Sorento tugged at her arm to move along faster.

"What the hell is bugging him, Stripes? He froze me out like I had a contagious disease."

Stripes didn't bother to answer the question. He just looked at Vance as his friend spoke. Vance had an uneasy feeling. What if Stripes had figured out his true identity?

"What the hell is bugging you now, Stripes?" Vance asked angrily.

Stripes stared at Vance before he spoke. "It's that thing you got hanging around your neck, Clicker -- the camera! I never really thought much about it before, but the few times I've seen you, you've always had that camera around your neck. I guess I got used to seeing it always hanging there, but Sorento noticed it right away and that's what made him freeze up. He thought you were going to take his picture, and in his business, he doesn't like any kind of publicity."

"What is his business, Stripes?"

Stripes evaded Vance's questions. "Why are you wearing that camera around your neck now? Do you have any film inside of it?"

Still doesn't trust me, thought Vance. "Naw," he paused, "I don't have any film in the camera right now. I shot it all this afternoon. I lost a good camera in the last pad where I lived. I don't want to lose this one too. That's why I'm keeping my camera and guitar with me all of the time -- wherever I go! You never know who's going to bust into your pad. So, you'd better get used to seeing me wearing the camera, because where I go, so does it with me too.

Stripes hesitated, then let out a loud bellow of laughter. "Come on Clicker, let's get going." He slapped Clicker on his back with the palm of his hand. They roamed the sidewalks together all night. Vance strummed the strings on his guitar and hummed a corresponding tune. Stripes would occasionally stop and talk with people sitting on porch steps, standing in doorways and sitting in parked cars. Vance stayed away when Stripes was conducting business, always playing the part of an uninterested bystander. Vance wanted these people to accept and trust him, and this was the best way to begin.

Vance assumed that all the people Stripes stopped and talked with were either pushers or addicts -- sometimes both. They decided to stop and get a bite to eat.

"Clicker," Stripes began the conversation, "the word's out that Sorento's having a big bash tonight at his pad. It really won't start rolling until about 11:00 p.m. How about going there with me? I'll be able to get rid of a lot of merchandise there."

Vance smiled and nodded his head in approval as he sipped hot coffee from the cup that he held. He needed something to settle his nerves before he entered his next adventure. It was soon to come and this was going to be his first real test.

CHAPTER 6

It was 11:30 p.m. Stripes and Vance walked up the entrance stairs of the old apartment building where Sorento lived. They stopped at the door. Stripes tapped out a rhythmical signal on the doorbell. "Just a little code Sorento and I cooked up," he said. He tapped out the signal code again.

Vance just nodded his head and looked over the surrounding area. Have to find out where we are, he thought. The house displayed no visible house numbers. Vance looked at a street post displaying a street sign. The sign was well illuminated by the street lamp above it -- *RISER STREET.*

Vance had to strain his eyes to read the numbers on the house directly across the street. Two-Twelve, Vance mumbled to himself. Then Sorento's house should be Two-Eleven South Riser Street.

The entrance door finally opened. Sorento stood in the doorway blocking entrance into his house. "It's about time you got here," Sorento snarled angrily, "we're almost out of everything!"

"Just take it easy. The *sweets* man is here," replied Stripes, trying to reassure Sorento that he'd be well satisfied with the quality and quantity of narcotics that he had brought with him. "I've enough goodies for everybody -- twice over."

Sorento turned and walked a few yards down a hallway. Vance and Stripes followed close behind him. Sorento suddenly spun around, grabbed Vance by his arm and pushed him against the wall.

"You ain't goin' in any of the rooms with that camera -- my friend." Sorento was furious.

"Relax, Sorento," interrupted Stripes, "that camera's got no film in it. Vance shot all of his film this afternoon. I know! I was with him. Clicker keeps that camera with him all of the time. It's his main gig to make some bread. He lost his other camera in his last pad. He doesn't want to take any chances on losing this one too." Stripes turned towards Vance. "Clicker, let him examine the camera."

"Anything you say Stripes." Vance nonchalantly handed the camera to Sorento. Sorento opened the back of the camera, looked inside, shut the small door, and handed the camera back to Vance. He

23

squeezed Vance's pockets to see if he was carrying any film with him. "I still don't trust him with that camera, Stripes." Sorento had a tone of annoyance in his voice.

They walked up half flight of stairs, made a sharp left turn and entered a large, drab painted room. The air in the room carried a foul odor mixture of burnt hay and body odor. A low hanging mist hovered over the heads of the people occupying the room. Everyone sat on the floor. They were a motley looking collection of men and women. A battered old phonograph, resting on top of an old cocktail table, blared out a chanting rhythm through its oval shaped speakers.

In the center of the cracked ceiling hung a mobile made from old pieces of scrap metal. It turned slowly, reflecting quick flashes of colored light from the Christmas color wheel illuminating it from below.

It took awhile for Vance to absorb the room's atmosphere. Some couples caressed. Others sat and stared into blank space mumbling unintelligible phrases.

A silhouetted figure got up off the floor, in the far most corner of the room and began dancing to the rhythmic beat of the music. The figure began the dance with slow and lazy movements, then quickly spun around, waving her arms in a wild frantic display. Vance recognized the dancer as she passed him. It was Monica.

Completely entranced with the music, Monica failed to notice Vance and Stripes standing in the doorway watching her dance. As the tempo of the music quickened, so did Monica's dancing tempo. She laughed loudly, occasionally screeching like a wild mountain lion ready to pounce on its' prey.

The music suddenly stopped. Monica fell to the floor in complete exhaustion. Beads of perspiration fell from her forehead. Her breathing was shallow and hard. She gulped in the few breaths of air that entered her lungs.

Sorento walked over to Monica, lifted her off the floor and carried her securely in his arms. He whispered something into her ear, but her lack of response was sufficient to show that she was completely unaware that he had spoken to her.

Sorento turned and left the room, still carrying Monica. Stripes walked into the room leaving Vance standing next to the doorway. He circled the room, stopping every now and then to talk with a person. Vance located an empty place to sit in one of the corners. He watched as everyone began changing partners. Vance tried to be as inconspicuous as possible.

A short while later, Sorento returned to the room alone. His eyes searched the room slowly, stopping when he saw Vance sitting on the floor. Vance knew he'd have to convince Sorento that he was using drugs. Vance looked hazily at Sorento and pretended he didn't notice him standing in the doorway.

Sorento headed straight for Vance and pulled the camera off his neck. He opened the back and looked inside. The camera was still empty of film.

The crumb still doesn't trust me, thought Vance. Sorento dropped the camera in Vance's lap and walked over to the other side of the room, first stopping to talk with Stripes. Several minutes later Sorento left the room again. Stripes made his way over to where Vance was sitting.

"Looks like you're in, Clicker." He shook Vance's hand.

"Yea," replied Vance, smiling. " I guess so." Stripes' face produced an unusual twisted grin, then he left the room. Meanwhile, couples entered and left the room in short intervals.

Somehow, I've got to put my film in the camera, thought Vance. It's now or never! If Sorento checks the camera again, I'm a dead pigeon -- but I've got to take that chance!

Vance made his way out into the dismal lit hallway. He located a bathroom at the far end of it. Once inside, he closed the door behind him and reached inside of his pant's waistband. He carefully removed a roll of very well hidden camera film. Opening the back of the camera, Vance inserted the film and connected it onto the gear wheels. Not wanting to leave any evidence lying around, he tore up the film wrapper and flushed it down the toilet. He adjusted the camera's lens opening, hoping that it would be adequate because of the small amount of light that was available. Leaving the bathroom, Vance went directly into the large room where the main body of couples had congregated. His luck was still holding out for him! His corner in the room was still unoccupied, and no one had touched his guitar.

Vance maneuvered his way through the room, stepping over bodies, finally reaching his corner. Bringing his knees up to his chest, he

25

sat in this position for quite some time. Occasionally he glanced up to see if anyone was watching him. Everyone seemed to be unaware that he even existed. When he was sure that it was safe, Vance began his *James Bond Adventure.*

Positioning the camera just below his kneecaps, he peered through the tiny range finder and took his first picture. He quickly photographed everyone that entered and exited the room.

Several hours passed. He realized that he hadn't seen Stripes for quite sometime. Certain that he'd photographed everyone in the room, he began his search for his missing roommate. Vance picked up his guitar and began his search in every room on the first floor. The occupants totally ignored him when he entered a room. They were preoccupied in their own drug induced dream worlds.

At the far end of the hallway, a staircase lead to the second floor of the building. Starting his walk up, Vance heard a horrifying scream that made his blood curdle. Fearing the thought of what he might find, he cautiously made his way up the stairway, stopping at the top of the landing. Several doorways broke up the pattern in the long pink colored hallway. Mumbling voices penetrated the doorway nearest to him.

Vance opened the door, just far enough for him to peek inside of the room. Fourteen people, dressed in black shrouds, occupied the room. In the center of the room stood two wooden altars, both covered with black, silk sheets. Imprinted on each of the sheets were symbols of the magic circle. The walls and ceiling were painted black with white Tarot symbols. Standing next to each altar was a large black wax candle resting on a wooden pedestal. On each altar lay a motionless figure -- an animal and a human being.

Eleven figures formed a semi-circle in front of the two altars. They were seated on the floor. Two persons remained standing -- one in front of each altar.

Vance recognized the fourteenth figure seated on the floor in the far corner of the room -- it was Stripes. A small conga drum rested between his knees. He beat out a simple rhythmic tempo using his fingers.

As the tempo began, the figures in front of the altars lit candles and chanted incomprehensible ritualistic phrases. A wooden model of Satan's head hung from the ceiling between the two altars. A wand made of hazelwood, a dagger, and a metal pentacle rested on top of each altar.

The two figures in front of the altars changed positions and walked behind the altars. They faced the congregation and removed the shrouds off their heads. Vance recognized both of the people -- Sorento and Monica. Their actions indicated that they were under some kind of hypnotic trance.

Sorento removed the black sheets from the altar tops. Vance beheld a horrifying scene before him. A young girl, lying on one altar, was partially beheaded. Her arm pits had been slashed, as was the crevices beneath her breasts.

A steady stream of thick red liquid flowed down her arm, falling into a large metal bowl on the floor below. Her eyes remained open, staring blankly at the ceiling above her.

Vance couldn't believe what he was seeing before his very own eyes! This was a witch's coven -- practicing black magic. In college he'd read several books on different human behavioral patterns for his abnormal psychology classes. Some of the books contained chapters covering the study of witchcraft -- just as it was happening here.

A witch's coven usually consisted of twelve women and one man. The man played the part of Satan in the ritual ceremony. The ceremonies consisted of simple prayers to Satan while they conducted animal and human sacrifices to him. Most ceremonies required that the participants be completely nude. Others required that deviate sexual acts, as well as sexual intercourse, be performed between the man and the twelve women at the conclusion of the sacrifices.

Sorento turned and faced Monica. She stood behind the adjacent altar. He picked up the black handled dagger off the altar and handed it to her. She slowly raised the dagger over her head, spoke several phrases, then swiftly brought the dagger downward, beheading a dog lying on the altar before her.

Monica picked up the blood soaked head with her hands, raised it over her head and let the droplets of blood decorate her face. She turned and handed the head to Sorento. He removed the eyes from their lifeless sockets and inserted a small black candle into each socket. He lit the candles and danced wildly around both altars.

Monica removed her blouse, revealing a pair of bullet shaped breasts. She raised her hands and wildly shook her head from side to side. Finishing her ceremonial prayers, she danced over to the young girl's lifeless body lying on the other altar. She thrust her fingers into each of the girl's wounds. Removing her blood soaked hands, she rubbed them around both of her breasts.

Monica danced and laughed hysterically. Each time she passed the dead girl, she thrust her fingers into an open wound, smearing more blood on her body and in her hair. Before long, she resembled a person who had been attacked with a butcher knife.

Vance felt like vomiting. Sure, he'd seen many dead bodies, but his training at the police academy didn't prepare him for this horrible scene. Instinct told him to push the door open and charge into the room, but if he did, he knew that his life wouldn't be worth a plug nickel. And yet, if by some remote chance of fate, the young girl was still alive, he could help her. Hell, this wasn't the time for wishful thinking. Calling for help now wasn't any good, it would blow his cover. All those months of preparation would be for nothing. Vance took his secret photographs of the room and all its' occupants. He wanted to capture as much of this fiendish crime on film as he possibly could.

Quickly unloading his camera, he tucked the roll of used film in the secret slot hidden inside the waistband of his pants. He made a decision. These bastards had to be stopped!

Vance turned quickly, to leave the building, but lost his balance. Hitting the door with his head and shoulder, it swung open and slammed loudly against the wall. Vance stumbled into the room and fell to the floor. The room became silent. Everyone watched Vance as he lay motionless on the floor. He had to act fast. His performance had to be a convincing one, because if it wasn't, he'd never get a second chance for a repeat performance.

Vance blinked and squinted his eyes, pretending that he was trying to focus his cloudy vision. He began moving his head swiftly from side to side. "*Stripes, are you in here*?" he screamed at the top of his voice. "*Where the hell are you? I can't see a thing. Everything's a blur.*"

Stripes stood up. "Here I am, Clicker. Over here!" Vance crawled on his hands and knees, purposely missing Stripes by several feet.

"Where are you Stripes? For God sake, help me," Vance pleaded. Luckily, Vance had struck his head on the door and the floor. He had a lump and a deep cut on his forehead.

"What happened, Clicker?" Stripes asked suspiciously.

"After I finished smoking my weed, I had to go to the John. I eventually found it. While I was taking a piss, I suddenly felt dizzy and fell, hitting my head against the damn sink. I must have been out for quite awhile. When I came around everything was one big blur. I've been wandering around ever since it happened, looking for you. I found the stairway and crawled up the stairs. When I reached the top stair, I heard voices. I found the doorway that the voices were coming from. I stood up and tripped on something, and fell into this room. Who's in here with you? What's going on Stripes? How come you're not downstairs with everyone else?"

Stripes didn't answer any of Vance's questions. He looked at Sorento who was listening attentively to every word that was being said. Sorento placed the animal's head on top of the altar and approached Vance. He again grabbed the camera from around Vance's neck. Opening the back of the camera, he examined the inside.

Vance ignored him. He stared down at the floor, mimicking a drug induced stuper. Still doesn't trust me, thought Vance. Screw him! Good thing I took the film out of the camera.

Sorento still remained silent. He shut the back of the camera and returned it to Vance's neck. He grabbed Vance's guitar and checked it over carefully, not really knowing what he was looking for. Sorento jerked his head towards the door, signaling Stripes to remove Vance from the room.

Stripes helped his friend off the floor and lead him out of the room. They entered another room at the far end of the hallway. Stripes helped Vance to lie down on an old army cot in the far corner of the room.

"Rest here awhile, Clicker. I've got a few things that need tending too, but I'll be back shortly and we'll leave."

"All right." Vance moaned, still trying to convince Stripes that he was in pain.

Stripes left the room. Vance laid still and listened. He could hear the shuffling of feet out in the hallway. Vance didn't dare try to see what was going on out there. He couldn't risk being caught again. He remained on the cot until Stripes came back for him some fifteen minutes later.

"How are you feeling now old buddy?"

29

"Fine," said Vance. "My vision is starting to clear up. Everything is coming back into focus again."

Vance got up off the cot. Both men walked out into the hallway. There was no one else around. As they passed the room where the grotesque ceremonies had taken place, Vance took a quick look from the corner of his eye. The room was empty. Everything was gone -- the girl, the dog, the altars, the candles, and all the people. Even the blood stain on the floor had been wiped clean.

Vance and Stripes hurried down the stairway. Monica and Sorento were waiting for them at the bottom.

"How are you feeling camera boy?" Sorento asked sarcastically. Vance remained silent. He stared directly into Sorento's eyes, hoping he would see the hatred that was there for him. Sorento grabbed Vance's camera again, opened it and looked inside. Once again Sorento was disappointed to find no film in the camera. Vance yanked the camera out of Sorento's hands. They left the building with Vance carrying his camera, and Stripes holding Vance's guitar.

It only took a short time for Vance and his roommate to get back to their room at the hotel. Stripes threw himself across the bed. It wasn't long before he was fast asleep.

Vance sat on an uncomfortable wooden chair, staring at Stripes as he innocently slept. How could he be a part of that? thought Vance. He tried to analyze the actions of his roommate. Stripes just watched a human life be destroyed with one swift sweep of a knife, and then came home and slept peacefully without even a trace of guilt for his part in that cold blooded murder. Vance just couldn't relate to this type of person.

Making doubly sure that Stripes was fast asleep, Vance removed a few objects from behind the old dresser: a pad of paper, pencil, envelope, and postage stamps. He had to get a report written for Captain Reese while the incidents of the night's activities were still fresh in his mind.

The report consisted of six hand written pages. Vance explained his operation and who his new roommate was. This was the first written report to Captain Reese since their first meeting in room 105.

Vance explained the sequence of pictures on the roll of film, listed the names of the people he had met, identified the house where Sorento lived, and listed the addresses. He also suggested that Captain

30

Reese match the photos that he had taken against the batch of photos that the department had of missing juveniles. He explained the ritual with the dead girl and explained his inability to help her. After outlining his future plans, Vance signed the report -- *TEDDY BEAR.*

He inserted the report and the roll of exposed film into a brown envelope and addressed it in care of T.B., room 105, City Hall. After applying sufficient postage, Vance put the rest of his writing materials back in their hiding place and went out to mail the reports before Stripes woke up from his nap and caught him with the envelope. So far, Vance had been lucky. How much longer his luck would hold out, he really didn't know -- he just prayed that it would...

CHAPTER 7

A week passed since Vance dropped the envelope into a United States mailbox. He and Stripes were sitting on a park bench. Vance stared blankly at the headlines in the newspaper he was holding.

The front page showed a picture of Monica and Sorento. Monica was draped over an overturned garbage can. Sorento's body hung half way out a second floor window. The printed columns next to the photographs explained the entire story:

"On complaints made by several neighbors, the
Police Department's Narcotics squad took action. Armed
with a search warrant, they raided the house at
Two-Eleven South Riser Street. During their investigation,
they discovered the partly decomposed body of a girl who
apparently had been murdered.

The main suspects in the case, a young man known
only as Sorento and a young women known only by the
name of Monica, were both killed while trying to escape
from the police. While climbing down the fire escape the
young woman slipped and broke her neck as she fell into
the alley directly below her. The young man smashed a
window and tried to escape by jumping through it. He
apparently lost his footing and fell on a jagged piece of
broken glass sticking up from the window pane and
punctured his throat.

31

The young slain girl was identified as a Miss
JoAnn Dean of Caver City, Michigan. The parents of the
murdered fifteen year old runaway made a positive
identification of the body and her personal belongings."

Vance took notice that no mention was made of the sadistic
ceremonial ritual in which the young girl was the sacrifice. Stripes
munched contentedly on a chocolate candy bar. "Too bad about
Sorento and Monica -- hey Clicker," he said smiling.

Vance kept quiet. He felt sorry for the young runaway girl who
had been slain for nothing but sadistic pleasure.

Times were starting to get rough out on the streets. Vance was
on his own without any kind of help or protection. If the time came
when he had to make an arrest, he had no weapons to protect him. He
needed a gun. Something small, he summarized, would be sufficient for
him. Maybe he'd get a woman's .25-caliber automatic. It was small
enough and he could attach it to the inside of his guitar. He could fasten
it in a way that it was concealed from anyone's view. Yes, Vance
decided that if he was to walk the streets alone, he'd have a weapon in
his guitar to help him out with any kind of a problem that he might
encounter. The next task on his agenda would be to get himself that
gun.

Vance stood up and crumpled the newspaper in his hands. He
stared at Stripes for what seemed like an eternity. "Yea -- it's just too
bad about them." He threw the crumpled newspaper into a metal waste
paper container as they walked out of the park together. The waste can
was a fitting resting place for trash like Sorento and Monica.

The following weeks produced great opportunities for Vance
to meet with several of Stripes' close associates in the narcotic's trade.
Vance's personal dislike for his drug pushing roommate grew more
intense each time he met a new friend of Stripes. Vance had finally
gained the trust of the people who lived in his neighborhood. No one
any longer paid any attention to the camera that hung around his neck.
At every available opportunity, Vance photographed everyone that he
was introduced too. He continued to write and mail his secret reports
to room 105 at City Hall.

With all this vital new information, it didn't take long for the new police unit to compile a complete file of records and photographs on local narcotic pushers, addicts, prostitutes, and runaway juveniles working and living in the area.

One afternoon, after finishing a well balanced diet consisting of two hot dogs with mustard, relish, and onions, furnished by the local fast food shack, Stripes suddenly blurted out a loud laugh for no apparent reason.

"What's the matter with you, Stripes? You've been acting funny all day. You've got something brewing up your sleeve. I recognize that goofy laugh of yours. It usually means you've got something special planned, so give with the info!" demanded Vance, really annoyed with Stripes' behavior.

"O.K. Clicker." Stripes wiped some mustard off his chin with his napkin. "Here it is. We've got a little caper planned for tonight. With all of the student unrest going on around the city these days, we figured that we should do our part helping the kids fight the establishment."

"We, Stripes? Just who in the hell is we?"

"Ricco, Ned and I are going to break into City Hall. We planned on destroying all the city records that we can find -- birth, businesses, marriage, tax, and any others that we can locate. Do you want to come along with us?"

"Are you nuts?" answered Vance. "You'll never get into City Hall. That building is buttoned up tighter than a metal drum full of high explosives. You're all out of your minds for even thinking about it."

"No--no," interrupted Stripes, "just listen Clicker. Ned has got it all figured out. It'll be a breeze. A few years ago, when he was in his last year of high school, Ned got a job as an apprentice janitor working in City Hall under the cities summer working youth program. He knows of a way to get into the building without being seen."

"What about the night watchman and the cop patrol on duty? Where'll they be while we're breaking into the building?" Vance was convinced that this was a stupid idea for them to try.

"The cops don't roam the building. There's only two of them and they stay in a little office all night long. The same night watchman has been working there for the last ten years. He takes the same lunch break all of the time. Ned knows his schedule backwards and forwards. I'm telling you, it'll be a breeze!" Stripes was convinced that the plan was fool proof.

"All right--all right," said Vance, throwing both hands up into the air. "Just suppose you're right about the plan. Explain just how it's going to work."

"What time is it now, Clicker?"

"9:45 p.m." said Vance after looking at his wrist watch.

"Listen," Stripes began, "I've got to meet Ned and Ricco at exactly 10:00 p.m. I don't have time to explain the whole plan to you. Why don't you just come along with us and see for yourself?"

Vance hesitated before giving Stripes his answer. He knew that he didn't have enough time to get in touch with Captain Reese so he could take measures to stop the break-in. If he went along with them, he might be able to do something to stop them without giving himself away, before they did any real damage.

"O.K. Stripes. Count me in. Let's go."

CHAPTER 8

The four young men met at the northeast corner of Lasalle and Washington streets at exactly 10:00 p.m. Vance had met Ned and Ricco a few times in prior weeks.

Ned was a revolutionary who hated everything that had a reason for existing. He demonstrated against anyone or anything -- for any reason. Ned loved to be with crowds. He'd get excited from the screaming and yelling coming from the people that were getting riled up.

His black hair hung straight, except for the upward curls at the bottom of the long thick strands. Ned stood over six feet tall and topped the scales at more then two hundred pounds. In his muscular hands, he carried a large carton.

Ricco stood next to Ned holding a medium sized duffel bag in his right hand. His chestnut brown long sideburns, and his handlebar mustache, helped to make his appearance exceptionally striking. The black sleeveless tee-shirt he wore revealed that he wasn't as muscular as Ned. Ricco never cared for demonstrations. He just loved to do any kind of destruction. Ricco especially loved to watch crews of men destroy large buildings, but most of all, Ricco thrived on the excitement that came with destroying something and not getting caught. This really got his rocks off.

The three men followed Ned into the alleyway directly in back of City Hall. There was no sign of movement anywhere. Even the alley cats hadn't started on their nightly prowl.

The men stopped in front of a large metal coal chute door mounted in the side of the stone building.

Ned looked at Vance. "That's the coal chute. It leads directly into the basement. It's a forty foot drop that goes down at a slight angle. See if you can open that door, Clicker," he said arrogantly.

Vance sensed that Ned liked to out wit the next guy when ever the opportunity arose. He was never happy unless he could outsmart somebody.

Vance bent down and felt the corners on the metal door looking for a spot to pry it open. After examining the metal plate for several minutes, he stood up and said disgustedly, "I can't find a way to open the door."

Ned laughed. "Let me show you how a real pro operates."

Ricco handed Ned a screwdriver. He inserted the tip of the screwdriver into the screw head in the lower right-hand corner of the metal door. Applying his weight against the screwdriver, he gave it a twist to the left. The metal door slightly sprung open. Ned inserted the head of the screwdriver into the small opening, applying pressure on it until the metal door finally gave way and fully opened. He looked up at Vance. "See that old buddy. Ain't no problem when you know how to do it. There's a spring release switch attached to the screw base. You have to turn the screw to the left and push in hard as you're turning to release the spring on the tension lever. Then all you have to do is lift the door until the lever bar slides into a slot and the door pops open for you."

"We can't go down that coal shaft," complained Stripes. "We'll get so filthy that it'll take a month of Sundays to get all of the dirt off of us."

"Don't worry about it," said Ned. "I've got it covered. Ricco, give me those plastic bags you've got in your duffel bag."

"Plastic bags? What are we going to do with them?" asked Vance.

35

"These are the large garden variety type leaf bags," answered Ned. "We'll climb inside of them. They'll cover us up to the top of our shoulders and we can slide down the shaft without getting ourselves dirty.

Stripes shrugged his shoulders and climbed into the first plastic bag. Ned and Vance helped him to get his feet into the small chute. He slid down the coal chute without a problem. Ned put several small cartons, containing aerosol paint cans, into a plastic bag and dropped the bag down the chute. Each man got into a plastic bag and followed Stripes down the coal chute.

The basement of City Hall was dark. Luckily, the building had been converted to gas heat and no coal was in the coal bins.

Climbing out of his protective bag, Ned switched on a small flashlight. The beam of light slowly crept along the brick wall until it found a flight of stairs that led up to the lobby of City Hall. At the top of the stairs, a large wooden door blocked their way into the lobby of the building.

Ned was the first to climb the stairs. The others followed him. Carefully turning the doorknob to the right, he felt the door give a little. He pushed with his shoulder until the door fully opened. Moments later they found themselves standing in the main lobby of City Hall.

The lobby was dimly lit, but adequate enough so they didn't have to use the flashlight to see. Vance was the first to speak. "What are we looking for? And please tell me what in the hell are we going to do with it when we find it?"

"We're not looking for anything in particular," replied Ned. "We'll start searching in that room over there, the one with the number *100* on it. We'll go from office to office destroying every file, in every cabinet, that we find."

Vance felt a strange tingling sensation run up and down his spine. Two nights before, he mailed an envelope containing his reports and developed photographs of Stripes selling narcotics to several addicts out on the streets. This was the first time that he had actually developed the photos himself.

The thought came to Vance that if Ned ever found that envelope in room *105*, he'd open it, look at the photos, and read the reports. After he did that, it wouldn't take a brain surgeon to figure out who had sent them to City Hall. Vance had to divert them away from room *105*, but it had to be done fast!

"Hey, Ned," Vance began, "why don't we just go upstairs to the teller's cages? We should find some loot up there. We sure could use that money more than just playing around with a stack of useless papers."

"We're not doing this for the bread, Clicker. Don't you understand? We're doing this for a cause. Our fight for freedom against this damn establishment."

The change of tone in Ned's voice showed his annoyance with Vance. Vance now realized that it was useless to talk to Ned anymore. He had to find another way to stop him. He couldn't let him get near room *105*.

Room *100* contained all the records for land registrations for both small property owners and large corporations.

"What a break," shouted Ned. "Destroying these records will really put this city into a state of turmoil. It'll take them at least three years to get everything back into proper order."

Ricco climbed up a ladder. He began yanking large ledger books off the metal shelves, letting them fall on the floor beneath him. Stripes grabbed a ledger and began ripping out pages from the inside of the book. Ned picked up a can of spray paint and started spraying the ledgers and stacks of papers laying in the center of the room.

Vance noticed another group of ledgers neatly stacked on shelving at the far end of the room. A fire alarm signal box was built into the wall next to the shelving. If I could get over to those shelves, he thought, I could stumble and set off that fire alarm. I'd make it look like I had an accident. The only problem is that when the firemen get here, so will the police. We'll all get caught, but I've got to do it anyway. I've got to stop them before they do anymore damage.

"Ned," said Vance, "there's another set of shelves at the other end of the room. I'll start ripping them apart."

"O.K. with me, but make God-damn sure you do a good job on them."

Vance walked to the other side of the room. He pulled a chair in front of the shelving and used it to stand on. He began pulling ledgers off the top shelf. When he was sure that Ned was watching him, Vance stretched awkwardly trying to reach a ledger and purposely lost his balance. His body slammed against the wall, sending his elbow smashing into the glass window on the fire alarm box.

Vance cried out in pain and spun around holding his elbow -- his eyes filling with tears. When his arm hit the fire alarm box, he quickly pulled down the signal handle. A throbbing pain ran up and down his forearm. How much damage had he done to his arm? he wondered. Upon examining it, he saw that a piece of broken glass had slashed his shirt and punctured the skin. Blood flowed freely from the open wound. Vance's partners ran over to see what had happened. Fire alarm bells were ringing loudly in all the hallways.

"*You stupid, dumb, clumsy, mother fucker!*" Ned screamed loudly. "*You just blew this whole caper for us.*"

"*I didn't blow it,*" screamed Vance, trying to stop the bleeding by applying pressure on the wound with his handkerchief. "We can still do more damage around here."

"No man. You blew it. You blew it good for us. The greatest caper we had going. We had a way to really fix the politicians and you had to go and fuck it up for us!"

Ned grabbed a telephone off of a desk next to him and raised it above his head. *"I ought to smash your fuckin' skull in with this damn phone -- you bastard,*" he screamed.

"*Hey, Ned,*" shouted Ricco.

"*What do you want?*"

"*The bells are ringing because Clicker set off the alarm when his elbow broke the glass and pushed down the signal handle.*"

"*Let's get the fuck out of here,*" yelled Stripes, already running towards the doorway. "*This place will be swarmin' with firemen and cops in a few minutes.*"

Stripes was to late with his warning. The police and firemen were already entering City Hall. Four uniformed officers appeared in the doorway of room *100*. The officers and offenders stared at each other for only an instant. Ned broke the silence. He yanked the telephone cord out of the wall and charged the officers, swinging the telephone wildly above his head. He looked like a contestant at a rodeo.

The heavy portion of the telephone slammed against the head of one of the officers. He collapsed to the floor instantly. Another officer tackled Ned and brought him down on his knees. Ned fought like a tiger and broke free from the officer's grasp. He started to get up off the floor, when a night stick smashed into his right shoulder, bringing him down for the second time. The sound of cracking bone was loud. Ned slumped into a state of unconsciousness from the violent shot of pain that found its' way to his brain. He laid motionless on the floor. The second officer drew his gun and pointed it at Ricco and Stripes. They froze in their tracks.

"Don't make any sudden moves," ordered the police officer. "I'm new on the job, nervous, scared, and will probably shoot if I'm provoked. Now, follow my instructions and nobody will get hurt." He paused. "Raise your hands up in the air with your arms stretched fully upward towards the ceiling." Everyone did as they were instructed. "Good! Now turn around and face the wall and assume the position. If some of you don't know what I'm talking about, spread your legs apart and rest your body on the balls of your feet and place your finger tips on the wall in front of you."

Ricco and Stripes followed the officer's instructions. Vance remained seated on the floor clutching his elbow tightly with his other hand. The officer turned and faced Vance -- his gun pointed directly at him. "That goes for you too pal," ordered the officer. "Get off of your rump and do what I said."

"I can't," replied Vance, "my arm is slashed and I can't stop the bleeding."

The officer signaled his partner to take a look at Vance's arm. At that moment the beat sergeant entered the lobby of City Hall and saw the group of men. "What have you got?" he asked. "Just what in the hell's going on here?"

"Got a couple of real bad jokers here Sarge, trying to destroy City Hall the hard way -- a page at a time," said the third officer. "We've also got a couple of hospital cases."

"I'll call for a squadrol." said the sergeant, "meanwhile, take those other two to the station and book them on criminal trespassing and destruction of property charges. I'll go to the hospital with the injured guys and see that the paper work gets started on them."

Vance decided on how he would handle the situation when they reached the hospital.

CHAPTER 9

The ambulance's siren wailed as it sped along the streets, going through intersections even though there was a visible red signal light.

Vance's arm throbbed painfully. The emergency room at Service Memorial Hospital was crowded with the usual Friday night emergency cases. Victims of robbery, assault, and tavern brawls occupied the chairs against the walls in the long corridor.

A young woman, sitting on a chair, was slumped over at the far end of the corridor. Her hands covered her face as she wept hysterically after being told that her husband had just died. He had taken their dog out for their usual nightly walk. A group of youths, driving by in a car, shot both him and the dog through the head -- just for kicks.

The squadrol backed up to the entrance door of the emergency room. Vance and Ned were rushed into the hospital by two officers.

The injured officer had already arrived at the hospital and was being treated for his head wound. Following a short wait, Vance and Ned's injuries were attended to by an intern.

Vance's wound required ten stitches to close it. Ned's right shoulder was broken in two places. The intern set it and applied a plaster cast, making his arm and shoulder immobile.

Vance was first to be approached by the sergeant. "All right, what's your name and where do you live?"

He desperately wanted to tell the sergeant that he was an undercover police officer, but he knew that this wasn't the right time to reveal his identity. Ned attentively listened to Vance's answers. He wanted to see his attitude towards the sergeant. "My name's *Teddy Bear* and I live in a big, dark, scary cave," was Vance's reply to the sergeant's questions. Vance displayed a smirky look on his face. He could see the sergeant's patience slowly slipping away.

"O.K. asshole," said the sergeant, "we'll put your name down on the booking sheet just as you told me. The judge always loves to get a smart ass like you before his bench. He'll know how to take care of you."

Ned spat out a loud roar of laughter that was cut short when the intern finished working on him, accidentally moving his shoulder. Hours later, Vance and Ned were transported to the district station and booked.

Early the following morning Captain Reese sat at his desk scanning over the log sheets of names of persons arrested the previous night. When he saw the name *Teddy Bear,* his eyes stopped searching the rest of the papers. He telephoned the district station where Vance had been detained and was informed by the desk sergeant that the offender was still in custody. Captain Reese instructed the desk sergeant to have Vance brought to his office for a formal interrogation.

An hour later Vance found himself sitting across the desk from Captain Reese. Neither person spoke for several minutes. Captain Reese sympathetically looked at Vance. His dirty clothes, long beard, unwashed scraggly long hair, and bandaged arm made Vance look like one of the street's underprivileged. Captain Reese finally broke the silence in the room.

"Having a pretty rough time of it, Officer Martall?"

Vance's expression of disgust revealed his inner most feelings about his undercover assignment. "Yes Captain, I've had one hell-of-a rough time," he softly answered.

"Does the arm hurt much?" Captain Reese was concerned about Vance's injuries.

"It hurts a hell of a lot. It took ten stitches to close up the wound."

"Tell me about it Vance, just what happened over at City Hall?"

"Ned, Ricco, and Stripes wanted to do some serious damage to the records at City Hall. They had planned on destroying all the records and official documents they could lay their hands on. I had to find a way to stop them. When I saw the fire alarm box, I got an idea. I knew that the police would come with the firemen as soon as I set off that alarm."

Captain Reese stood up and walked over to the window. He remained silent for several minutes, watching the cars pass by the building in the street below. Finally, he turned around and spoke.

"Up until now, Officer Martall, you've done one hell-of-a job. The reports and photographs you've supplied to us in the past months, have helped tremendously in making arrests, and gathering other valuable information on people and places of vital importance. You also

41

did an exceptional job in helping us wrap up the murder of that teenage girl on Riser street."

"Why couldn't I have helped her?" asked Vance. "Captain, why couldn't I have gotten there just a few minutes sooner? If I had, maybe she'd be alive today." Vance's voice unveiled a pleading and protesting tone.

"You can't stop every crime from happening, Officer Martall," said Captain Reese with a stern voice. "Don't blame yourself for her death. She was most likely dead way before the time that you saw her body."

Vance didn't reply to the captain's statement. Captain Reese sat down at his desk. Several more minutes of silence dominated the atmosphere in the room. Again, Captain Reese was the first to speak.

"Officer Martall, the Mayor realizes the many hardships that you've had to endure in the past months. He's asked me to tell you this. If you feel that you want to end your assignment, all you have to do is to say so! If you request that it end, you'll be returned to regular duty and reassigned to a district station. The decision is entirely yours, but before you make that decision, I'd appreciate if you'd let me add my two cents on the subject. Out there in that jungle is a never ending problem that has to be fought. In the short time that we've been operating this special unit, we've just scratched the surface of that problem. And you -- you are the vital key to the whole operation. Without you, we might just as well disband this unit."

Vance realized that *now* was his chance to get out of this lousy assignment. He thought, I wouldn't have to live, eat and deal with Stripes and his kind anymore. I could go to a regular station and wear clean clothes again. I could return to a normal way of living. All of these thoughts kept running through his mind -- repeatedly.

Vance was ready to tell Captain Reese his final decision -- he wanted the assignment ended.

Before Vance could speak, Captain Reese opened a brown portfolio and removed the contents. He handed them to Vance.

"What are these?"

"Reports and photographs of an incident that occured early this morning. Read the reports and examine the photos," said Captain Reese. Vance began to read:

> "At 3:00 a.m. this morning, the narcotics unit
> conducted a raid of a house at 1426 South
> Williams Street. Inside one of the apartments

they found six dead persons -- four males and two females."

Vance stopped reading the report. He wanted Captain Reese to explain it. "What happened to them Captain? How did they die? Who were they?"

"They were just ordinary teenagers around seventeen and eighteen years of age," sadly answered the captain. "They died from a combination of two elements: an overdose of heroin and a deadly mixture used for cutting the heroin. The crime lab analyzed some of the heroin that they found with the bodies and discovered that the heroin was cut with a large doseage of Brazilian Tumage. The drug drove the kids out of their minds."

"What was the name of that stuff again Captain? Tumage you called it? I never heard of it before."

"It's a substance that comes from the back country of Brazil. Basically it's a white powder that paralyzes the central nervous system and forms a blood clot inside of your brain. Those kids were so far under the influence of drugs that none of them knew what was happening to them.

"A preliminary autopsy showed that the main artery, that feeds blood to the brain, burst, once the blood clot settled in the brain. We're trying to track down their supply source as fast as we can. This was to be your next assignment. The supplier is either a maniac or just a sadistic killer who gets his kicks from knowing what'll happen to the people who use his mixture. In either case, Officer Martall, he has to be found and stopped as soon as possible."

Vance stood and walked over to the window. Looking at the captain he said, "You know Captain, the Mayor was right when he said that there was a wild jungle out there in those streets. He really didn't know how right he was. Right now, as I look through this window, I can visualize thick, green foliage with trees growing close to each other in the streets below. Did you know that the slang word these kids use for a hypo needle is *Spike*. Right now I can visualize various colored pills growing on bushes and hypo needles hanging from the branches of trees, just free for the taking. That's what's out there -- *A Spiked Jungle* with a *Diabolic Populous* doing the devils work by preying on the innocence of the young."

Vance turned and faced Captain Reese again. He knew now what his answer was to the Mayor's question. He had to finish what he started. There was no turning back now. He couldn't desert the unit. The only way out for him was either discovery or death, and that would end all his worries.

"Captain Reese," Vance began, "would you tell Mayor Cotagney that I'll continue on with my undercover work. Tell him I'll stop only when I've completed this assignment, I'm discovered as an undercover cop, or I'm dead."

Captain Reese nodded his head and smiled. "I'll tell him just that way, Officer Martall. Just exactly the way you told it to me."

"Now that we've got that settled," said Vance walking away from the window, "just where do we go from here? What happens now?"

"You'll be returned to the jail where your other three partners are at."

"Back to jail?" remarked Vance, a tone of disbelief in his voice.

"I know it's a lousy break Officer Martall, but that's the way it has to be. You'll have to go back to jail and be with the others so you won't draw any suspicion. We've already contacted the judge who'll be handling your case in court. We've explained our situation to him and he's agreed to go along with us. We had to take him into our confidence. He'll cooperate. Because of your clean records, you and Stripes will only receive a ten day sentence in the County Jail. The other two have previous arrests and convictions, and they'll receive a longer jail sentence."

"What about all the damage that was caused at City Hall?" asked Vance. "Just how bad was it?"

"Fortunately, the damage that was done was minor. The ledgers that were destroyed were only duplicates. The originals are still in a vault in the second sub-basement of City Hall. In fact, special city employees are already beginning to work on them now. They're Xeroxing all of the pages"

"Well, that's that then."

"I'm afraid so Officer Martall. I'll have you transported back to the district station. We won't let you post a cash bond, so you'll be sent to court the first thing tomorrow morning. When you're standing before the judge, you'll plead guilty and will accept the sentence that the judge gives you. Immediately after your sentenced, you and your buddies will be removed to the County Jail to start serving your sentences. When you get out, your main concern will be to locate the person responsible for that bad batch of poison that's out in those streets."

"Won't my ten days in jail just be a waste of time?" Vance hesitated. "I mean, if it's so important that I locate this person as quickly as possible?"

"We have information that the only time this bad heroin shows up on the streets is when the street supply is almost exhausted. That's when someone starts pushing the bad stuff. Our informants tell us that a fresh supply of heroin will hit the streets tonight. This supply should last about twenty or twenty-five days before it's all gone and the addicts are looking for a new source. We'll do our best to try and grab every kilo of heroin that's coming into the city. It should make a lot of people desperate and open up a clear field for you to operate."

"Wow," said Vance, shaking his head, "I sure hope your plan works."

Captain Reese rose from his chair. He shook Vance's hand, applying a firm grip as he smiled. "Good luck, Officer Martall. And I really do wish you -- good luck!"

Vance had an uncomfortable smile on his face. No one had to tell him it would take even more luck than he'd had so far, if he was to come out on top, and alive from this assignment...

CHAPTER 10

Ten days in jail seemed like an eternity for Vance. In the early morning hours of the eleventh day, Vance and Stripes were released from County Jail. As they exited through the jail's entrance gates, Stripes turned his head, spat at the brick wall, and stuck up his middle finger at the tower guard at the same time.

"That's in honor of my ten day stay here," Stripes snarled angrily.

"Does it make you feel better to spit at a plain brick wall?" said Vance, laughing as he spoke.

"Hell, I do feel better already," replied Stripes. "Well," he paused, "where do we go from here?"

"Let's go back and see if we still have a pad to bunk down," said Vance, looking for the bus stop.

A blanket of darkness had covered the city when Vance and Stripes finally reached Kelter Street. They walked up the staircase in their hotel, along the dim, dusty hallway, and into their dirty room.

Once inside, Vance sat down on an unstabled chair by the table. Stripes plopped himself down on the bed.

There was a loud crunching sound. Stripes stood up and removed a blanket that was concealing a smashed guitar. "Holy shit Clicker, I'm sorry about the guitar. I'll buy you a new one," said Stripes apologetically.

Good thing I didn't place that automatic weapon inside of the guitar, thought Vance. I'd have a lot of explaining to do. "Don't worry about it. There's a lot of them at the pawn shops." Vance felt bad about Paco's guitar.

Both men remained silent for a long time. Vance spoke first, breaking the silence barrier. "All right Stripes -- give!"

"Give what, man? I don't know what you're talking about?"

"Listen," snapped Vance, "you're using straight horse. We just spent ten days in the cooler, yet you come out of there without so much as a twitch. What gives? How did you do it?"

Stripes turned and looked directly at Vance. He burst out in laughter. Vance became furious. He was becoming very annoyed with Stripes' habit of constantly laughing at him whenever he asked him a question. It made him feel like an idiot.

"O.K. Stripes, just cut out all the bullshit." Vance was angry. "Just tell me how you did it?"

"Don't get so uptight, Clicker. I'll tell you everything, only cool down that temper of yours. Just before we went down that coal chute, I got rid of the narcotics that I had, along with my metal shell necklace. You remember that live shell that I carried?"

"Yea, I remember it -- go on."

"I stuffed the shell and the narcotics into a crack I found in the brick wall. I didn't want to have any of that stuff on me in case something got fouled up and we got caught."

"So what. So you hid a batch of powder inside of a brick wall. That still doesn't answer my original question."

"All right, let me show you how I did it." Stripes inserted his right index finger and thumb into his mouth and removed a plastic, partial dental plate. On the upper portion of the plate, that clung to the roof of the mouth, was an oval, flexible shaped sack that resembled human skin.

"See this," said Stripes, showing Vance the dental plate. "This is where I always carry my emergency supply of drugs, just in case I'm somewhere that I won't be able to get any. There's enough drugs in this

46

sack to last me for quite a long time. When we were being checked in at the receiving room in the jail, the guard spotted the old track marks on my arm and asked if I was still on the hard stuff. I told him that I was clean and he believed me. He never bothered to search me any further. He passed me through.

"I felt all right the first day, but around supper time of the second day it started to get to me. I stole a small spoon from the mess hall and borrowed a book of matches from the guy sitting next to me. After lights out, I took the plate out of my mouth and opened the sack. I had all of the makings that I needed. All I had to do was sit in the corner and face the wall so that the guard wouldn't see the glow, from the burning match. I cooked my drugs in the spoon. When the right temperature was reached, I swallowed the drug. It takes a little longer to reach the blood stream, but it does the same job in the end."

"Yea," interrupted Vance, "but you didn't have enough drugs to last you the whole ten days."

"I wrapped the remainder of my drugs in some toilet paper and tucked it inside of my mattress." Stripes continued. "Remember the day that I had a special visitor?"

"Sure, I remember. You told me that some broad came to see you."

"Right. Her name's Rea. I ran out of drugs at the end of the third day. I spread the word around and I was contacted by one of the inmates. He told me that he knew how to get the drugs into the jail if I had enough dough to pay for it and his services. He wrote down a name and address for one of my friends on the outside to contact. It cost me a good piece of change, but it was worth it.

"When Rea was here, I passed on the information to her and told her how much to pay them. The next day, I got enough heroin to last me the rest of my time in jail. That, my good friend, is how I survived the terrible torture of the establishment's prison," said Stripes.

Vance said nothing, letting Stripes think that he had accepted Stripes' explanation. This kind of information had to get back to Captain Reese. It was always suspected that narcotics were being smuggled into the jail, but not being sold on such a wholesale basis. Captain Reese would be very interested with this information.

Vance thought, who was this girl called --Rea? How did she fit into this operation? In all the time that he spent with Stripes, he had never heard Stripes mention this girl's name, and yet, she just pops up

47

out of nowhere and produces a lot of money for Stripes to buy narcotics. It had to have cost him a small fortune to have those drugs smuggled into the jail.

Vance had to know more about this mysterious girl. Somehow, she was an important link in Stripes' past, which they had never really discussed in detail.

"Stripes, who's Rea? You never mentioned her name before."

Stripes wrinkled his brow and looked up at Vance displaying a serious expression on his face. "Clicker, we've known each other for quite some time now. I've been watching on how you reacted in all types of situations. In fact, I've watched you very closely."

Vance was very well aware of the truth of Stripes' last statement. "I think it's about time you and I had a long talk -- man to man or friend to friend. Maybe we really should get to know one another a hell of a lot better," Vance suggested eagerly.

"What should we talk about?"

"You know, talk about our past lives. Maybe, a little more in detail. Like, who's Rea? Stuff like that."

This was it! Exactly the moment that Vance had been waiting for. Could be he had hit pay dirt at last? He had to be careful about the questions that he asked and the information he gave out about himself.

"Rea's a very important part of my entire organization," Stripes boasted proudly.

"What organization?" remarked Vance.

"Don't let the long hair and weird clothes fool you. Rea and I were very good friends before I went into the military service."

Vance was surprised at the last statement. "What branch of the service were you in?" he asked.

"The Marines. I did my basic training at Paris Island. After I finished boot camp, I was stationed stateside for several months."

"Were you hooked on drugs when you joined the Marines?"

"Not right away." Stripes continued. "While I was stationed stateside, a rebellion broke out in Brazil. My outfit was sent there at the request of the Brazilian government. Our mission was to protect the American citizens that were living there. The Brazilian militia wasn't adequate enough to handle the situation with all of the unrest in the country."

Brazil! thought Vance. Maybe Stripes *is* the person that I'm looking for after all. The only thing is that these killings, using bad drugs, just doesn't fit Stripes' style of doing things -- no -- not Stripes.

"While I was down in Brazil," Stripes continued, "I was involved in a bad automobile accident. The truck I was riding in blew out a front tire and went out of control as we were starting to go down a long steep mountain road. The truck rolled over several times as we went down the side of a mountain. The truck kept turning over as it fell down a tree infested mountain side. We finally stopped turning over. There were ten of us riding in the truck. Two of us survived." Stripes paused for a second and then continued. "I survived and a kid from Indiana who was thrown out of the truck when we first started to roll over. Almost every bone in my body was broken. The pain was unbearable. I wound up unconscious.

"When I awoke, I was lying in a hospital bed. The doctors kept me heavily sedated so I wouldn't feel the pain. The condition that my body was in didn't give the doctors much hope for my recovery. Because of this, they kept me on a large dosage of morphine. For several weeks it was touch and go for me. Finally, I began recovering very slowly.

"The doctor's started reducing my dosage of morphine, but of course, by that time I was already hooked on the stuff. I was in agony again, but this time it was from the lack of the drugs. A Brazilian nurse took pity on me and gave me an extra booster shot of drugs each night so I could sleep. When I left the hospital I located a local pusher who took care of my needs while I remained stationed in Brazil.

"It was over a year when I finally got shipped back to the States. I contacted Rea and told her about my drug problem. She told me that she'd help me. At that time she was working as an assembly line worker in an electronics parts factory. Rea spread the word around on what she wanted and it wasn't long before she was contacted by one of her fellow workers.

"My needs got more frequent and more costly, so I decided to go into business for myself. Rea and I discussed my idea and she agreed to go along with me. After all, I had a lot of good contacts in Brazil. Rea worked as my personal secretary as well as being a full time partner -- as she still is now."

This is it. I was right, thought Vance. It's either Stripes or someone else in his organization that's pushing the bad drugs.

49

Stripes continued. "Remember that first night we met, Clicker?"

"I sure do. That was one hell-of-a run we did to get away from the police."

"Do you remember that radio I was carrying under my arm?"

"Yea, why?" replied Vance, a puzzled look on his face.

"When you threw that radio down that chimney, you destroyed about forty thousand dollars worth of the best and purest grade of heroin."

"What!" exclaimed Vance.

"The heroin was packed inside metal tubes attached to the chassis of the radio." Stripes continued explaining. "A shipment of both radio parts, as well as fully assembled radios headed for the United States, originally started out from a port in Hong Kong. The transporting ship made a brief stop in Brazil to refuel, unload and pick up cargo, and let passengers off the ship. My contact in Brazil discovered a way to get some our cargo aboard the ship. He premarked a few wooden packing crates that contained the narcotics. He mailed that radio to a small shop that I operate at the far end of Kelter Street."

"What's the name of the shop?" Vance showed extreme interest in Stripes' explanation.

"The *Small Clock & Radio Fix-It* shop. I picked the radio up at the shop that night. In my haste, I forgot to wrap it when I left the shop and two cops riding in a squad car saw me come out of the shop. They turned on their spotlight and headed directly for me. I guess they thought that I stole the radio. Anyway, I couldn't let them catch me with the drugs, so I made a run for it. That's when I ran into you.

"When we were on that roof top and you tossed that radio down the chimney, I was ready to throw you down the chimney after it. I didn't because the cops were almost on the roof. So you see my friend, you owe me exactly -- forty thousand greenback dollars.

"*You're nuts,*" shouted Vance. "*Forty thousand dollars? Where in the hell am I gonna get forty thousand dollars? You're out of your fuckin' mind pal. Just where in the fuck do you think I'm gonna get that kind of bread to pay you?*"

"That's easy. From now on, you're on my payroll."

"Doing exactly what?" inquired Vance.

"You'll receive a regular weekly salary, plus there'll be extra jobs for you to do for me. I'll pay you a good wage for each special job you handle. That money will be deducted from the forty grand that you owe me. You see Clicker, that's why I've stayed so close to you. I want my forty grand and I'm going to get it back from you, either in cash, or in services."

It all worked out so easy for Vance. Stripes was forcing Vance to stay with him. He couldn't have thought of a better plan himself.
"All right Stripes, I'll work for you. I'm with you all of the way. Where do we go from here?"

"I've been looking for a good right hand man for quite sometime now. I needed a man that I could really trust. You're that man, Clicker. You're going to be out there in those streets making contacts for me. I'm getting off the streets. I want to start expanding my organization's connections. I've had to work the streets myself, wearing this get up, so I could keep my customers supplied and happy. I couldn't really trust anyone except myself, that is, until you came along.

"I'm moving out of this hotel room today. I have my own apartment uptown. I'm gonna get myself some new threads and a haircut today. You'll keep on living here. If you need anything, just let me know and I'll get it to you."

"Will I still have time to take pictures with my camera?"

"Sure. Just as long as it doesn't interfere with my business operation. You'd better understand one thing right now, Clicker. I don't want anything or any hobby to get in the way of my business."

There was still one question that bothered Vance and he had to know the answer before Stripes left the apartment. "Just one more question, Stripes."

"Ask away pal."

"That partial dental plate gimmick of yours is bothering me. What kind of material is that plate made of and how do you stop the drugs from seeping down your throat?"

"That was another of my earlier investments. I accidentally came across two young college kids a year ago. They'd been living in this area for only a month. We met in that small diner at the corner of Twelfth and Summit Streets. We discussed a lot of things. One of them asked me if I knew of anyone who wanted to invest some money in a possible profit making proposition. I told them that I might be interested, that is, only if it sounded good to me.

"Convinced that I was sincere, they told me that while they were in school, working in the physics lab, they accidentally stumbled on to an interesting new substance. After mixing several grams of many different chemicals, both liquids and powders, one of the students accidentally knocked over a vial containing the new concoction into a

51

bowl of specially treated water. The result of that accident is the substance that is used on top of the partial dental plate.

"When they finished telling me their story, I decided to back them financially for other future experiments. I had the money, and they furnished the brain power. Their first project was making the dental plate, and they finished that with flying colors.

"The sack, on the top portion of the plate, is as flexible as human skin. The amazing thing is that liquids won't soften or dissolve the material, and it can't be punctured."

"Well, when you need the material inside of the sack, how is it opened?"

"There's a tiny air bubble in one corner of the sack. I have a secret substance that will separate the corner of the sack from the dental plate. The funny thing is that the secret substance is made up of everyday house hold products. Once the seal is broken and the outside air enters the sack, I can lift up the corner and remove the contents from inside the sack.

"What are the household products that you mix to break the seal?" asked Vance.

"Oh, never you mind my friend," replied Stripes, "that too is still a secret."

"Can the sack be resealed once its been opened?"

"No, that's the problem they're working on now. The only way to get a sealed sack, is to remove the old one and attach a new sack to the dental plate. The drugs have to be protected from damage as the substance is poured over the drugs and attaches itself to the plate, concealing the drugs. The drugs are sealed in rubber. As the substance dries, the sack is sealed, burning up all of the oxygen inside of it, giving you a vacuum sealed sack."

"What other projects are they working on?" inquired Vance, his interest growing more intense. "What other goodies have they come up with? Where's their lab located?

"Hey, Clicker," said Stripes, becoming suspicious at all the questions being asked, "how come you're coming up with all of these questions, all of a sudden? Why are you so concerned about the *Why's* and *Where's*?"

Oh--oh. Better cool it, thought Vance, or I'll blow this whole deal for sure. Got to play it by ear and see just what happens. "Hey pal, no sweat," replied Vance, placing his hand on Stripes' shoulder. "I just got a little excited over all the possibilities of that new discovery. Can you imagine the dough that it could bring in for us."

"That's exactly what it's doing right now for me," Stripes replied, smiling devilishly.

"Huh?" exclaimed Vance.

"Never you mind, Clicker, that's enough talk for now. I've got to leave, but I'll be in touch with you in a couple of days. Stay around and just sit tight. Take your pictures or find yourself a broad to keep you busy."

Stripes stood up. Reaching into his front pant's pocket, he removed a large roll of money. He counted five fifty dollar bills off the top of the roll and handed them to Vance. "Here's your first weeks pay."

"Where did you get all of that dough? You were broke when we got out of jail and came here."

"I had it stashed inside of this mattress. I put it there some time ago."

Vance took the money without hesitation, counted it and tucked it into his pant's pocket. He didn't say a single word. Stripes twisted a rubber band around the roll of bills and tucked them away in his pocket. Stripes left the room. He walked down the hallway and stopped at the head of the stairway. Turning around, he looked back at Vance standing in the doorway of the room and said, "You can do one favor for me, Clicker."

"And what's that Stripes?"

"Do you remember that picture you took of that little brunette in that bikini?"

Vance had a questionable expression on his face.

"You remember," continued Stripes, "the day we were at the beach. You took the picture through the bottom of a broken bottle. It was great the way her large assets stood out -- even larger than normal."

"Oh yea. I remember that day now. What about the picture?"

"Man, every time I think about that picture, it gives me a hard on! Could you blow me up a copy of it so I can hang it on the wall in my apartment?"

Vance laughed. "Sure Stripes, sure. Anything for a pal."

"Great Clicker, and thanks," yelled Stripes as he ran down the stairs, *"see you in a couple of days."*

Vance went back into his room. It was time for him to do some serious thinking, but first, he had to get his reports written for Captain Reese and mail them. At last, he finally was making some real progress. He was actually brought into the center of his roommate's operations. He knew that the further he got in, the more difficult and dangerous his job became...

CHAPTER 11

Vance remained in his room the entire first afternoon of his new job -- doing absolutely nothing. Came night time, he decided to take a walk around town and take some pictures. A lot of new people had joined the living populous in the local area. Many faces were totally new to Vance. The younger generation had migrated into the local area quite heavily during the past weeks.

Vance stood on the sidewalk waiting for the traffic light to change. A police patrol car screeched to a stop in front of him. Two uniformed officers got out of the car and approached Vance, both carrying their wooden night sticks.

The taller of the two officers spoke first. "Put your hands on the roof of the car and don't try anything funny."

Vance obeyed. One officer gave Vance a quick search while the other officer stood back and watched them. Vance was puzzled. Why had these officers single him out from the crowd of so many people walking around? "What did I do?" he asked, his hands still on the car. "What do you want from me?"

"Just face forward and shut-up," ordered one of the officers, removing the camera from around Vance's neck. He removed the camera lens and examined it closely. "This is one of them," he said to his partner, confident that they had made a good arrest. "Here's one of those identifying marks."

"What are you talking about?" asked Vance. "What kind of mark? What's going on here? Who are you guys trying to railroad? Listen, I'm clean. I haven't done anything wrong for you two to bother me. All I have is a camera and was going to take a few pictures."

The officer, pointing his gun towards Vance, removed a pair of handcuffs from a leather pouch attached to his belt. He fastened

Vance's hands tightly behind his back. The officer started to inform Vance of his rights, but Vance interrupted him. "All right, I know what my rights are. Just tell me what in the hell I did wrong?"

"We've been looking for you for several days now," replied the officer. "My partner and I saw you walking around this neighborhood several times in the last few weeks. We saw you taking all those pictures with this camera. We figured that you were taking photos of the stores for possible future burglaries. You know, studying their weak points for when you were ready to break into them. My partner also suggested that the camera might be hot, so we decided to check you and the camera out. This is the first chance we've had to get you.

"This camera was taken in a burglary from the *Belton Camera* shop. It's one of a hundred cameras that were stolen from there. Mr. Belton had a special trade make stamped on several parts of the cameras before the factory shipped them to him. It helps, in situations such as this, to be able to identify the stolen merchandise."

The officer's partner called for a squadrol to transport Vance back to the district station house.

Vance remained silent, although troubled inwardly, cursing his rotten luck. Damn it, he thought, I forgot all about the camera being hot. I've got to get out of this somehow. Everything was going just fine for me. In a couple of more weeks I could have finished this assignment and been back in uniform.

It only took a few minutes for the squadrol to arrive to transport Vance. A crowd of people had gathered around them to see what was happening. Vance was sure that someone in the crowd would recognize him and get word back to Stripes about the arrest, but in the meantime, how was he going to get himself out of this mess?

The squadrol, with Vance as a passenger in the back, turned the corner and went directly to the district station's parking lot. Vance was quickly removed from the squadrol and escorted down a drab painted hallway. The three men entered an interrogation room. One officer remained with Vance while the other officer went to the sergeant's desk and picked up an arrest report. He returned to the interrogation room and sat down in front of a typewriter. "Take the handcuffs off, Mack," he said to his partner, "and have him empty his pockets on top of the table."

Once the handcuffs were removed, Vance obeyed the officer's orders. The entire contents of his pockets consisted of a dirty handkerchief, a key to his room, two rolls of exposed camera film, thirty-five cents in United States coins, and five fifty dollar bills.

"Wow, will you look at that," remarked the officer sitting in front of the typewriter. "Just where in the hell did you get all that money, fella? What kind of work do you do?"

Vance didn't reply. He sat on a wooden bench staring at the floor.

"Mack, take all of his things and inventory them," said the officer writing the report, "and inventory the camera too." The officer continued typing out Vance's arrest report. "O.K. pal, what's your name?" he asked, looking at Vance.

Vance still remained silent.

"*Hey fuckhead. I said, what's your name,*" shouted the angry officer.

"*Teddy Bear,*" Vance snapped back his answer.

The officer typed *Teddy Bear* on the arrest report, then hesitated and stopped typing.

"Hey, aren't you one of the guys who tried to bust up City Hall a few weeks ago?"

"Yea, I'm one of them -- so what?"

"Well...well...well. What do you think about that. You must like our jails, coming back here so soon," said the officer laughing as he continued typing out the arrest report.

Several hours after Vance had been fingerprinted and photographed, he was told that his lawyer wanted to see him. Vance was taken to a room, where a man whom he had never seen before sat in a chair next to a small table.

As Vance entered the room, the man stood up and introduced himself. "Mister Clicker, I'm Thornton Downs, Aaron Cook's personal attorney."

"Aaron Cook?" remarked Vance, "who in the hell is Aaron Cook?"

The attorney smiled as he sat down. "He's the man you know by the name of Stripes, Mister Clicker."

"Cut out that mister bullshit, pal," snapped Vance. "Just call me Clicker. So Stripes' real name is Aaron Cook."

"Yes, Clicker. Mister Cook called me as soon as he heard that you had been arrested. He instructed me to see what I could do for you to expedite your dilemma out of this situation.

56

"*Do for me?*" shouted Vance angrily. "*You can get me out of this fuckin' place! That's what you can do for me.*"

"Take it easy. Be patient, Clicker. Everything takes a little time. Now, tell me just why were you arrested?"

"The police said that I had a stolen camera in my possession."

"Did you steal the camera?"

"Hell no. I didn't steal no camera. I bought the damn thing from a pawn shop across the street from where I live. Can't you post bail for me so I can get the hell out of this jail?"

"For some reason, they're not letting you out on bail right away. I've got a message for you from Mister Cook. He wants you to co-operate with the police in every way possible. He also wants you to tell them anything that they want to know about that camera. I'm going to leave now, but I'll call the station regularly to see when you're eligible for bonding. When you're ready, I'll post the bond and you'll be released. Mister Cook wants to see you as soon as you're released."

"O.K., just cut all the bullshit and get me out of here, fast."

The attorney stood, picked up his briefcase, walked to the door, and called for the guard. As soon as he left, Vance was taken back to his cell. Two hours later, Vance found himself sitting in a chair in front of Captain Reese.

"All right, Officer Martall, tell me what happened."

"It was just a rotten piece of bad luck, Captain. Two beat men picked me up on a street corner. I had that hot camera with me. What about that pawn shop? Was the tip that I gave you any good?"

"Yes, very good in fact. He's a good fence. One of the biggest in town. We didn't even know about him until you discovered him."

"Did you close him down yet?" asked Vance.

"No, we're waiting till we're sure he has a full load of hot merchandise. We're ready to move in any day now."

"Do it today, Captain. By shutting him down today, it may turn out to be a big help for me."

"What do you mean, Officer Martall?"

"Stripes is the head of a large narcotics organization here in the city."

"What?" exclaimed Captain Reese, astounded at what he had just heard from Vance.

"That's right," replied Vance, "and here's some more hot information. Stripes' real name is Aaron Cook. He was in the Marines and was stationed in Brazil. I feel very confident that either he or

57

someone else in his organization is mixing and pushing that bad batch of heroin."

"Yes, you're right, Officer Martall. This was a very bad time for you to get arrested. We'll have to figure a way of getting you out of this situation."

"It's really not as bad as we think , Captain."

"What do you mean?"

"I had a visit from a lawyer, that Stripes sent, a few hours before I was brought here. He told me that there was a hold on me and I wasn't eligible for bonding."

"They held you for interrogation on request of this office," explained the captain. "I'll notify the station that it's all right to bond you out. By the way, we found more dead kids in an alley early this morning. They were all using the bad drugs. The supply of good heroin must be getting low because the bad drugs are starting to appear on the streets again. You don't have to much time to clear this case up."

"I know Captain, but I'd like some information about another subject that's been bothering me," said Vance.

"Sure, go ahead and ask."

"Have you had a large number of burglaries in the past few months?"

"It's funny that you should bring that up. I was reading over this report on my desk when you were brought into this office. There really hasn't been an unusual amount of burglaries or robberies, but the total amount for the month is noticeably higher than last month's totals. Also, the Detective Division sent me a report that's very interesting.

"Two weeks ago, the lab technicians began to get very lucky. An unusually large amount of latent fingerprints were suddenly being left at crime scenes. The lab technicians photographed and lifted the impressions and sent the results to the fingerprint people in the Latent Unit of the Identification Section. All the latent print impressions had patterns that were exceptionally clear in all of the cases involved."

"My explanation for that," interrupted Vance, " is that a group of amateurs are working in the area."

"Wrong, Officer Martall," interrupted the captain. "Here's another interesting bit of information. One of the latent print examiners recognized one of the latent impressions that was brought in for comparison work. It so happens that he testified in a case just a few months ago involving the same identical fingerprint pattern. The man that those fingerprints belong to was convicted of burglary and was sentenced to the state prison."

"Maybe he committed the burglary while he was out on an appeal bond?" suggested Vance.

"Wrong again, Officer Martall. The man entered the state prison exactly two days after the end of his trial. We checked with the prison warden and he verified that the man in question was in fact still in their custody. Our latent print people then checked the other latent prints and discovered that the latent prints found at all of the crime scenes belonged to people who were already in jail doing time. It was impossible for them to have committed the crimes themselves.

"The night before last a watchman was shot and killed when he interrupted a burglar. The killer left the murder weapon on the floor next to the watchman's body. The Crime Lab technicians retrieved a beautiful set of latent prints off of the barrel of the gun. The serial numbers on the gun had been filed off. After an extensive search through our fingerprint computer, the fingerprint pattern on the murder weapon was found to belong to a man who's been in state prison for the last eighteen months. Everyone's puzzled. The police commissioner's up in arms and wants this case solved as soon as possible. Every available man has been placed on this assignment."

An idea suddenly came to Vance. Captain Reese noticed the unusual expression on Vance's face. "Do you have some information that can help us regarding this case, Officer Martall?" he asked.

Vance explained about the conversation that he and Stripes had back at their hotel room. He mentioned the new material that had been discovered and filled Captain Reese in on what was happening at the county jail. When Vance finished, Captain Reese picked up the telephone and dialed a number. He spoke for a few minutes, then hung up the phone.

"Officer Martall, the information that you've just given me may be the answer to our problem. That was the Commissioner that I just had a conversation with. He's instructed me to get you back on the streets as soon as possible. He feels just as I do. You're our principal link in solving these unusual crimes that have occurred these past few months.

"The Commissioner wants you to get in touch with Aaron Cook as soon as possible. Try to find out the location of his laboratory. It's essential that we get this information right away. If Aaron Cook and the chemists decide to sell this information on the open market using a bidding process, then the method we use today for identifying criminals with fingerprints, would become completely obsolete and useless. All criminal defense attorneys would have a field day in the courts. Did Aaron Cook ever talk about telling this secret to anyone else beside you?"

"No, Captain Reese," replied Vance, trying to remember all of his past conversations with Stripes. "As far as I can remember, the only people who know about the discovery are the two inventors, Aaron Cook, and myself."

Captain Reese rubbed his chin with his fingers. He looked at Vance and said very sternly, "You'll have to find out for certain that the only people who know the secret of that new material, are in fact the people that you just mentioned. It's very crucial that you do. We'll have to keep a twenty-four hour surveillance on everyone that we find involved with this new discovery. I'm going to have you transported back to the district station, but keep in touch with us every time you get a hot piece of information."

CHAPTER 12

It only took a short time for Thornton Downs to get to the police station and post a cash bond for Vance's release. They left the police station together walking to the attorney's car.

"All right Downs, where do I go from here?" asked Vance, acting very arrogant

"Mister Cook wanted to see you at his apartment as soon as you were released," replied the lawyer, keeping his composure.

"Fine," replied Vance, "but please tell me just where in the hell does he live?"

"Don't you know?" replied Thornton Downs, surprised.

"If I did know asshole, I wouldn't be asking you for his address, now would I?"

The lawyer resented Vance's rude attitude. He didn't care for Vance's choice of words, nor the tone of voice he chose to use when he spoke to him.

Thornton Downs felt that this hoodlum should have a little respect for his profession, if not for him. The only thing preventing him from taking a poke at Vance was the hundred-thousand dollar a year retainer that Aaron Cook was paying him to be his attorney. Reluctantly, Thornton Downs scribbled Aaron Cook's address on a piece of paper and threw it at Vance.

Thornton Downs opened the door of his car and sat down in the driver's seat. He didn't utter another word to Vance. He started the car and drove off, heading in the direction of his Gold Coast apartment.

Vance laughed quietly to himself as he read the address on the scrap of paper -- 1210 Denville Drive, apartment 1610.

He knew this section of the city very well. It was one of the plushest residential areas in the city. Only the most prominent people lived there. Somehow, Stripes was accepted in that upper class community without question. What respectable profession was Stripes engaged in to fool all of those wealthy people?

The apartment building was only a few miles from the police station, but it was to long of a walk for someone who was really feeling bushed.

Vance walked to the corner and waited at the bus stop. It was only a short wait before the cross-town bus pulled up in front of him. Vance pulled himself up into the bus and deposited a few coins into the coin box. Locating a seat that looked comfortable and inviting, he sat down, leaned back, and closed his eyes.

I'll just rest for a little while. The bus must be ahead of schedule, he thought as the bus moved along slowly. He tried to erase all the events from the previous months from his mind. He just wanted to rest, but his efforts were useless. Everytime he tried to forget, everything kept coming back to him -- *Stripes organization, poisoned heroin out on the streets, the young girl killed at the sacrificial ceremony, mysterious fingerprints popping up at scenes of crimes, kids lying dead in alleys from using bad drugs.* All these little bits of information kept spinning around in his head.

The bus finally reached Vance's stop. Getting up from his seat, he pulled the signal cord. The bus came to a full stop. Vance pushed the exit door open and jumped down to the sidewalk. He surveyed the surrounding area and quickly located the building he was looking for. It took only five minutes walking time to reach it from the bus-stop, but Vance took his sweet time getting there. He wasn't that anxious to meet up with Stripes -- not so soon again. Each day, his association with Stripes grew increasingly bitter.

A burley and husky doorman guarded the entrance door leading into 1210 Denville Drive. He courteously opened and closed the large doors for the people entering and exiting the large building.

Vance slowly strolled up the curved cement sidewalk, stopping at the large glass entrance doors. He began to open the door when a muscular hand grabbed his arm, temporarily immobilizing it. Holding tightly onto Vance's wrist, the six foot-six inch doorman gruffly asked, "And just where in the hell do you think you're going -- *Gutter Bum*? Got some idea about jackrolling one of the tenants in the building?"

Vance's temper hit the boiling point. He felt his face flush as his heart began to beat rapidly inside of his chest. Vance clenched his fist tightly bitting hard on his bottom lip until it started to bleed.

The doorman's facial expression reassured Vance that if he didn't give the right answers, he'd possibly have a broken wrist, arm or most likely -- both!

"Hey man, cool it," said Vance, forcing a smile. "I'm just here visiting a friend of mine, that's all."

"What's the name of the person that you know who lives in this apartment building?" asked the doorman.

"Stri----." Vance caught himself before he said Aaron Cook's street name. "I'm here to see Mister Aaron Cook."

The doorman released his grip on Vance's wrist, letting the blood circulate back into his arm again. He still watched Vance with a suspicious eye. "Don't you move from that spot or I'll bust every bone in your body," ordered the doorman, still pissed off at Vance.

Walking over to the telephone hanging on the wall, the doorman lifted the phone off its holder, dialed a few digits and waited. Vance remained motionless.

"Mister Cook, this is James the doorman. I've got a bum standing here next to me who insists that he's a friend of yours. Yes -- yes sir. What's your name?" he asked Vance.

"Just tell Aaron that Clicker's here!"

"This character says that his name is Clicker sir. Yes sir, right away." The doorman hung up the phone. "Mister Cook wants you to go right up to his apartment."

Vance displayed a devilish smile as he gave the doorman an *I-told-you-so* snicker as he started to open the large glass entrance door.

The doorman stopped Vance. "Look gutterbum," he bellowed, "I told you before that you weren't going upstairs by way of this entrance elevator. There's a freight service elevator in the back of the building -- use it! The sight of you riding in these front elevators would make the respectable people living in this building vomit."

Vance broke away from the doorman's grasp. He cursed him inwardly as he searched for the entrance door leading to the freight elevator. The alley was dark, except for a dimly lit doorway. Vance opened the door and walked into a small vestibule. Blotches of dried mucus decorated the walls and floor with an uneven pattern.

Vance pressed the call button and waited, wondering what he'd find upstairs...

CHAPTER 13

The doors closed slowly. The elevator crept upward towards the sixteenth floor of the building. Stepping off the elevator, Vance entered a plushly decorated hallway. Stripes stood in the doorway of his apartment waiting for Vance to arrive.

"Whataya say, old buddy." He laughed as he greeted Vance. "How goes it with you? Why did you come up in the freight elevator?"

"Ask that damn bull dog you got down stairs guarding the front entrance of the building," snapped Vance, really pissed off.

"He's all right, Clicker. He just takes his job a little to seriously, but he's good at his work, and he's dependable too. Come on in and make yourself at home. There's someone inside that I want you to meet."

Stripes led the way into the apartment. Vance followed. The apartment was lavishly decorated. Collectable articles could be seen everywhere. This was the other side of Stripes' personality and lifestyle that Vance had never seen before.

Vance's eyes stopped admiring the living room when he saw a seductive looking red headed woman curled up in a white and black fur fabric lounge chair. The woman wore a dark blue satin dress that revealed enough front cleavage to make any man start panting.

"Rea, I want you to meet someone special to me," said Stripes. "This is the guy that I was telling you about. Clicker, this is Rea."

"Hi, Rea," replied Vance, trying to be friendly.

Rea slowly looked up from the book that she was reading, gave Vance a quick once-over look, and went back to reading her book without uttering a single word. It didn't take a genius to figure out that she was totally uninterested in Vance or his presence in their apartment.

"Aaron shouted, "*REA!*" Without looking up from her book, she shouted back, "*He's dirty, Aaron!*"

Stripes was furious with Rea's hostility towards his friend. He stormed over to where she was sitting, yanked the book out of her hands, and threw it against the wall.

"*Listen bitch,*" he screamed, "*this is the guy that I picked to help us with the organization. He's gonna handle all of our street connections. You're going to see a lot of him from now on because all of the meetings are going to be with you when I'm out of town, and that's going to be most of the time. Now get off of your lazy ass baby, because you're no better than any of us here in this fuckin' room. We're in this profession with one objective in mind, and that's to make money -- lots of fuckin' green folding paper money.*

Rea crawled out of the lounge chair and adjusted her tightly fitted dress. She looked at Vance, held out her hand and forced a smile.

"Hello. What was your name?" she asked condescendingly.

"Clicker." Vance took hold of her outstretched hand.

"Hello, Clicker," she replied, acting totally bored.

Stripes smiled and nodded his head in approval. Rea pulled her hand away from Vance's grasp and walked over to the portable bar. She removed a bottle of bonded bourbon off a shelf, opened it, and poured the entire contents of the bottle over her hand that had touched Vance's hand. She looked at Stripes. "That fuckin' creep looks like he hasn't taken a good bath since the last time he got lucky enough to get a good fuck. Why don't you take him to a car wash and just walk him through? That should get him super clean," Rea walked passed them. She went directly into the bathroom, slamming the door shut behind her.

"Pay no attention to her, Clicker. Now and then she gets into one of her highbrow moods. She's really O.K. Come on, let's sit down and talk."

Vance sat down on the couch. The bathroom door swung open. Rea stormed out of the bathroom and walked through another doorway without taking notice of the two men sitting on the couch.

"Where is she going now?" asked Vance.

"That's her bedroom."

"You mean she lives here with you?" Vance tried to visualize the sexual relationship between her and Stripes.

"Sure." Stripes pointed to another room. "That's my bedroom over there, just opposite hers. It works out better this way. This apartment is actually the center of our operation. By her living here with me, I never have to worry about trying to locate her when I need her for something special to do for me."

"What about you two--ahhh--getting intimate? Doesn't it bother you to have her here with you all the time?" Vance was anxious to hear the answer.

"Like I told you once before Clicker, our sexual attraction for each other ended years ago. This is strictly a business venture for the both of us. By her being here, helps my organization's chances for expansion. Now, let's forget about Rea and get on with some of the important business that I got you up here to talk about."

"O.K. with me," replied Vance, "when are we going to your lab so that I can see just how that special material is manufactured?"

"Never mind about that special material for now." Stripes was getting annoyed with Vance's questions. "You'll get to see that operation soon enough. First of all, I want to go over our narcotics distribution procedure with you."

"O.K., man," said Vance, laughing, "go ahead and get it off your chest."

"First, here's the telephone number for this apartment." Stripes handed Vance a piece of paper. "Most of the time someone will answer when you call. I have an answering machine that's connected when I know that no one will be here. Just follow the instructions on the tape when you call and leave your message. I'll eventually get back to you."

Vance folded and tucked the piece of paper into his front pant's pocket. Stripes removed a large sheet of paper from a brown portfolio lying on top of the cocktail table and handed it to Vance. "If you read along as I explain what's on that piece of paper, you'll find it easier to understand."

Vance nodded his head in approval and began reading as Stripes continued talking. "In the extreme left hand column you'll see that there are thirty addresses. Those are the addresses for your deliveries. You'll receive an envelope of money each time you make a delivery.

"The second column on the paper indicates the day of the week that you'll have to be at that particular address. For example, next to the first address there's a series of numbers: one, three, five, six and seven. Each number stands for a certain day of the week. Number one is Sunday. Those numbers are the days that you'll be at those addresses. The third column on the paper indicates the time that the meeting has to take place. You're not to be there earlier and you can't be no more that five minutes late, or the buyer will be gone. The time element is written out according to military time. That's from 0001 hours to 2400 hours. Do you understand everything that's been explained so far?"

`"Yea, I think so. It sounds simple enough. Do we follow this same schedule all the time?"

"No! Rea works out a new schedule every month. We don't like to follow a straight routine pattern in our operation. The last week of each month, Rea will mail out new lists to all of our special customers."

"What about your other regular customers?"

"Don't worry about them. They'll all be taken care of!"

Oh -- oh, thought Vance, I did it again. I'm pushing to fast with my questions. I've got to be more careful.

"You know which people I'm talking about? Those people you met all those weeks we were together out in the streets. You weren't shaking hands with them merely as a social gesture. I figured you were passing drugs to them," said Vance.

Stripes smiled. "You figured that out all by yourself -- huh, Clicker! You were watching me all the time after all."

"Sure I was. I saw what you were doing, but I could care less. It was none of my business. If that's what you wanted to do, it was no skin off of my nose."

Stripes continued. "Don't worry about them. As you go along, you'll pick up more strays and you'll be their supplier. You'll work out your own meeting places with them. Their kind of business is strictly peanuts. The real meat and potatoes is on that list I gave to you. That's why I want you to understand everything that's on it -- O.K.?"

"Sure." Vance was anxious to keep Stripes talking. "What's next?" he asked.

"As I said before, I want you to still live where you're at now. By the way, just what in the hell did you get locked up for this last time?"

"Didn't your lawyer tell you when he called you?"

"He just mentioned something about you having some stolen property in your possession."

Vance pointed at his bare neck. "Do you remember that camera I always carried around my neck?"

"Say," interrupted Stripes, "that's what's missing. I've been trying to figure out just what was so different about your attire. Your camera is missing!"

"Yea," Vance continued, "well, I bought that camera from that pawn shop directly across the street from the hotel. The camera was hot. I forgot all about the damn thing being stolen. Anyway, two cops picked me up while I was standing on a corner waiting to cross the street. The cops checked the camera out and found some kind of special code stamped on it. They took me in and booked me."

"What did you say to the cops when they questioned you?"

"I told them exactly what your lawyer told me to say. I told them the truth about that damn pawn shop."

"Good," replied Stripes, "serves the bastard right for selling hot merchandise. Did the cops believe you were telling the truth?"

"Of course they did or I wouldn't be sitting here talking with you right now. By the way, how the hell am I gonna beat this rap? I've got to be in court in three weeks. I just finished doing time. When that judge gets me in front of him again, he'll throw the book at me this time. I'll do more then those ten days."

"That's why I told you to co-operate with the police. As long as the detectives know that you were telling the truth, they'll go to bat for you when your case comes up in court. You should end up with a court supervision sentence or a short probation period -- at the very most.

Vance threw Stripes a sarcastic look. "I'm glad you're so sure of my future. Oh, never mind. Let's just go on with the rest of the list. I've got a few more questions about this set-up."

"I'll answer all of your questions in due time Clicker, but first how about a drink or maybe a bite to eat? I should've offered you something when you first got here. That little incident with Rea made it slip my mind."

"I'll have a whiskey and water," said Vance, smacking his lips together. "Never mind the food."

Stripes stood up and walked behind the portable bar. He pulled out a towel from the bottom drawer of a cabinet and wiped the puddle of whiskey off the top of the bar. Taking two clean glasses off a glass shelve, he filled them with ice cubes and set them on the bar. Stripes broke the seal on a new bottle of bourbon and poured until each glass was half full. Lifting a pitcher of cold water, he filled the remainder of each glass and gave them a quick stir with a swizzle stick. Opening the door of his bar refrigerator, he removed two glass jars filled with chilled shrimp buried in a red cocktail sauce. Stripes twisted the lids off the jars and dumped their contents into a large glass bowl decorating the top of the bar.

"Come on over and sit here at the bar, Clicker. Bring that piece of paper with you. We'll continue our discussion over here."

Vance walked over to the bar and perched himself on top of a bar stool. He removed a tooth pick from a small plastic cup and speared a large shrimp. Popping the shrimp into his mouth, he chewed slowly, totally enjoying each morsel of flesh. After swallowing the shrimp, Vance continued with his questions. "Does Rea always go and sit in her bedroom when you've got company?"

"Naw, just when the bitch is pissed at me," answered Stripes, laughing. "*Hey Rea!*" he shouted, "*are you gonna come out here and give us the pleasure of your wonderful company?*"

A firm but angry voice replied from behind the bedroom door. "*Get fucked! You bastard!*"

Stripes laughed again. "I guess she's really pissed off at me this time."

Vance shrugged his shoulders and took a sip of his drink. "Let her sit and sulk, Stripes. Let's go on with our discussion. First of all, where do I pick up the drugs? How much will I receive each time? Where will I keep them? What's the selling price? And how do I know if I'm meeting the right person when I make the contact?"

"Here's the set-up." Stripes placed his half empty glass on the bar. "You'll pick up the packages here from Rea. You'll make a pick up every three days. The most you'll receive at one time will be a half dozen one-pound bags of heroin and two hundred tin foil packets."

"How am I supposed to move around carrying all that stuff?"

"I'm getting you an old beater car just for that purpose. It'll be in perfect running order, but the outside will be dented and rusted so as not to attract to much attention. You'll store the drugs in your hotel room before and between deliveries. Don't worry about the selling price on the one-pound bags. The customer will be informed about the price when we send him his monthly contact list. The contact will give you a sealed envelope when you make the delivery to him or her.

" Don't open any of the envelopes. Bring them directly here after you've completed your run for the day. I trust you and I'm not worrying about you tapping the till. If there's a shortage of money when I open the envelopes, I'll know who to deal with personally. As far as the foil packets go, they're selling for a ten spot apiece. I'm going to give you an extra half-pound packet of pure heroin to cut yourself. You can use that half-pound to give to the clients you'll pick up as you go along. I want you to remember one very important thing. And again I emphasize, each time you complete making your daily pickups, you're to bring the money here to this apartment.

"Now, as far as making sure that you're meeting the proper contact, I've added more information to that code sheet that you're holding. I've found it necessary to add two extra columns to the list until you learn what the contacts look like and how much each one gets of the merchandise. One column will give a code word that they'll say to you and you'll reply with a preset answer."

"Whoa! Hold on now!" interrupted Vance, holding both hands up in the air. "Let me go over this sheet of paper once more. The first column is the address where I meet the contact. The second column of numbers represents the day on which I make contact. The third column is the time that we're to meet. The fourth column shows the amount of merchandise they get. The fifth column gives the code word they're to say to me and the last column is my reply code. Right?"

"Perfect! Right down to the last detail, Clicker. You've got a good head on your shoulders. You catch on fast. That's why I picked you to work for me. We're gonna make a great team -- Rea -- you -- and me."

Vance enjoyed the taste of a few more shrimps, then finished the rest of his drink.

"How about another one?" Stripes picked up the bottle of bourbon.

"Naw, I'll pass this time," declined Vance, "it's getting kind of late and I'd better be on my way. I'm beat and I sure could use a good nights sleep."

"Why don't you just bunk down here for the night? There's plenty of room."

"Naw," Vance declined the offer, "I don't want to impose on you and Rea. By the way, when will I start working on that list schedule?"

"Next week, Clicker. It'll be the fist of the month and I'd like to start you out with a fresh monthly list. I'm going to finish out this week myself. Drop by next Saturday night and Rea will give you the new list and packages of drugs. Your car will be parked downstairs in front of the building. Rea will give you the keys and the registration for it."

Vance jumped off the bar stool. "Good," he remarked, "then I'll be back here next Saturday night." Walking towards the front door, Vance shouted in the direction of Rea's bedroom. "*Good night, Rea! It was a pleasure meeting you!*"

A voice, shouting from behind the bedroom door, firmly replied, "*Drop dead prick!*"

Stripes slapped Vance on the back, laughing hysterically at Rea's remark. "You really made an impression on her." He stopped laughing and reached into his front pant's pocket and pulled out a fifty dollar bill. Handing the money to Vance, he said, "Maybe you ought to go out and buy some new clothes -- and maybe take a bath too."

Vance remained silent. His eyes shot Stripes a look of anger as he grabbed the money out of his hand. Vance stormed out into the hallway and headed directly for the back freight elevator. He didn't tell Stripes -- *Thank You* or *Good-By*e -- when he left.

Vance didn't dare take the regular passenger elevator down to the first floor, for fear of what would happen to him if by chance he got caught by the bulldog guarding the front door.

The freight elevator finally reached the street level. Vance walked out of the freight elevator, through the rear exit door and out into the dark alley. The night air felt cool and refreshing as it brushed against his face. He reached the end of the alley and walked out onto the sidewalk. He inhaled deeply, letting the cool, crisp fresh air fill his lungs. For some unknown reason, Vance lost all of his feeling of weariness. He felt like just walking.

It wasn't long before he realized that he was walking on the street where he lived. He entered his hotel and climbed that long flight of stairs that he'd climbed so many times in the past months.

As he entered his room, he turned on the light, walked over to the sink and turned on the cold water faucet. The cold water felt great against his face. He looked for a rag or used paper towel to dry his face, but there was nothing available. He finally used the tail portion of the shirt that he was wearing. Vance removed the writing materials from their secret hiding place and began preparing his report for Captain Reese.

After finishing a complete rundown of the day's events, he concluded his report with an explanation of Stripes' distribution program. He sealed the large envelope containing the reports, wrote down the customary address on the envelope, applied special postage, and went out to mail the envelope so it would be in Captain Reese's hands the very first thing in the morning.

Vance returned to his room and went to bed early. He wanted to get plenty of rest. He knew he had gained Stripes confidence, but he'd have to be twice as careful with Rea -- of this he was certain. The thought of it made him somewhat apprehensive...

CHAPTER 14

The loud wail of screaming sirens woke Vance back to the world of reality, early the following morning. He leaped out of bed and ran over to the window. The street below was filled with police vehicles -- Mars lights flashing and sirens wailing. People gathered on the sidewalk trying to see what was happening. Regular beat cars, unmarked detective cars, and large police vans blocked off both entrances of the street. Uniformed and plain clothes' officers went into the pawn shop and guarded all entrances.

Moments later, the owner of the pawn shop was brought out of his front door with his hands handcuffed behind his back. Two officers walked him over to one of the waiting squadrols, placed him inside, and locked the door securely. Within minutes, officers began carrying merchandise out from the pawn shop, loading it into the cargo areas of the other large waiting vans.

Vance smiled thinking, it's about time the Captain pulled a raid on that place. This should get my charges dropped when my court case comes up.

He wanted to check on his financial status before he proceeded with the next step of his project. Much to his surprise, he had accumulated two hundred fifty-seven dollars and sixty-five cents. He had to buy a new camera if he was going to continue being useful to the department, but this time the camera had to be legally purchased. He couldn't take another chance on getting caught with another hot item.

The first thing of the day, on Vance's agenda, was to buy the new camera. If he had any money left, he'd get himself some new clothes, a haircut, and a shave. Scooping up all the money, he tucked it into his pant's pocket. He had many chores to take care of, but feeding his stomach came first. The regurgling cries of hunger could be heard -- as well as being felt.

The waitress removed the empty dishes from Vance's table. He smiled, letting out a loud belch of satisfaction. "That was a compliment for the chef," he said to the waitress when she turned around and looked at him. She turned and walked into the kitchen with the dirty dishes. Now to begin my purchasing spree, thought Vance.

The camera shop was his first stop. Vance picked out a 35mm camera with automatic selector settings for focus, distance, and lighting. The bill came to exactly one hundred and six dollars. He still had enough money to buy himself some clothes. The store next to the camera shop was a haberdashery store. A large white paper sign, with black and red lettering on it, was taped to the glass window announcing the store's special sale.

Vance opened the store's entrance door and walked in. The store was fairly crowded with potential customers. A few men were trying on jackets, while others decided what colored shirts they wanted to purchase.

Vance checked out the items in the store, while he waited for a salesman to wait on him. Several salesmen looked at him, but completely ignored his existence. Vance was well aware of just what was taking place in the store. The salesmen didn't want to wait on him because of the way he was dressed -- and smelled.

A man, much smaller and thinner than Vance, stood next to a glass counter at the far end of the store. The passing years had reduced the amount of hair on the top of his head, leaving only a salt and pepper fringe to caress the back of it. Vance approached the man and started off the conversation. "Say Chief Bald Eagle, can you help me out?" he asked. Vance had taken the gentleman by surprise, leaving him standing with his mouth wide open.

"What do you mean by calling me, Chief Bald Eagle?" the salesman angrily replied. "Do I look like an Indian to you?"

"Take it easy pops," said Vance laughing. "The American Eagle's just as bald as you are, and that's what you remind me of with your bald head and beak shaped nose -- an eagle. Just take it easy. Don't get your feathers ruffled."

"What are you looking for?" asked the salesman.

"I need a whole new outfit." Vance removed a pair of pants from the clothing rack..

"How much do you have to spend?"

"About a hundred bucks," snapped Vance.

"O.K., what will you need?" asked the salesman as he opened his order book and began writing down Vance's requests.

"A pair of pants, underwear, tee-shirts, socks, a pair of shoes, a jacket, and two shirts." Vance told the salesman what his sizes were for the various items and what colors he preferred. The salesman selected all the clothing, with Vance's approval, and stacked everything neatly on top of the glass counter top. He added up the cost of all the merchandise. "That'll be ninety-eight dollars and forty-two cents young man."

Vance counted out a hundred dollars and handed the money to the salesman. When he received his change, Vance asked, "Have you got a fitting room where I can change my clothes?"

The salesman pointed to a doorway in back of where he was standing. "Go right through there," he said, pointing, "you'll find several small fitting rooms -- use any one of them."

Vance followed the salesman's instructions and walked into the first cubicle that he came to inside of the fitting room. Finished with putting on his new clothes, he left the fitting room, leaving his old clothes on the floor. "Take care of those," he told the salesman, then left the store.

His next stop was the public bath house, where he showered and scrubbed down several times to make sure he was really super clean. Satisfied with the washing results, he located a barber shop that was glad to accommodate him. Vance had his long hair trimmed and styled. A brightly colored, beaded headband encircled his forehead tightly so his hair wouldn't blow around freely. His face was clean shaven, except for a beautifully styled mustache on his upper lip and a neatly shaped Van Dyke beard on his chin.

When the barber was finished with his task, Vance got out of the barber chair and stood in front of a full length mirror, admiring himself. He was well satisfied with the results of his afternoons busy shopping venture. He wondered what Rea would think of him now. Well, he knew he wouldn't have to wait long to find out...

CHAPTER 15

Vance felt, in different ways, like a changed man. The bath, clothes, and haircut had done wonders for his ego. The rest of the afternoon passed quickly for him.

As night time approached, Vance decided to try out his new camera. The heavily populated area on upper Klauser Street was the ideal place for taking his photographs. There was always plenty of people milling around, and the lighting from the neon signs was perfect for obtaining the unusual pictures he was seeking.

Vance photographed couples taking leisurely strolls, examining shop windows, and just sitting around doing nothing. He was surprised at how popular he had become. Instead of shying away from him, everyone actually wanted to pose for him. Everywhere he went people greeted him with friendly smiles and handshakes. Word had evidently gotten around about his close relationship with Stripes and his organization. Vance and his camera were both accepted.

Saturday night. Vance saw a junk yard runaway, 1969 four door Ford Sedan, parked at the side of Stripes' apartment building. He stopped and examined the car carefully -- checking out both the interior and exterior, as well as the engine. The doorman, seeing Vance bending over the engine, ran over to the car.

"*Hey!*" he shouted angrily. "*What are you doing to that car? It doesn't belong to you!*"

Vance looked up at the doorman and casually smiled. "I'm not doing anything to the car. I'm just looking it over."

"Say, haven't I seen you around here before?" The doorman carefully examined Vance's face. "Sure, I know who you are now. You're that character that got so damn smart with me the other day."

Vance backed away from the car and began talking rapidly, hoping to convince the doorman of his honesty. "I was only kidding around with you. This is my car. Mister Cook picked it up for me. I'm on my way up to his apartment to pick up the keys and car's registration."

The doorman's demeanor softened slightly. "I see you got yourself a new set of duds along with a fancy haircut and shave."

"Yea. Looks great on me, doesn't it?" replied Vance jokingly as he turned around in a circle, so the doorman could see the back of his outfit too.

The doorman ignored Vance's comment "Mister Cook instructed me to send you right up to his apartment when you got here."

"And did Mister Cook say what elevator I was to use this time?" asked Vance, trying to sound as if the whole misunderstanding was nothing but a big joke.

"Mister Cook said that if you were presentable I was to let you go up by way of the front elevators."

"Well now, good fellow, do I pass your personal inspection?" asked Vance sarcastically.

"Yea, you can go up the front way."

Vance slammed the hood of the car shut and headed for the front entrance of the building. The doorman walked beside him. When they reached the entrance door, Vance stopped and waited. "Well?" he asked.

"Well what?" asked the doorman.

"Aren't you the doorman?"

"Sure I'm the doorman -- so what!"

"So open the God-damn door for me. I'm a guest here, ain't I?"

Vance quickly side stepped the doorman's massive hand as it flashed passed his stomach and grabbed the handle on the door. The doorman whipped open the door, and held it open until Vance had walked through it. As Vance walked by, he winked, and bowed his head reverently, saying "Thank you master." The doorman's face turned red with anger.

That'll teach him to bruise the back of my neck, thought Vance, stepping into the elevator. It quickly sped up to the sixteenth floor. Vance stepped out of the elevator, walked over to Stripes' apartment door, and knocked.

"Just a minute," came a reply from a feminine voice behind the closed door. The doorknob turned slowly. The door opened with Rea standing there blocking the doorway. She was wearing sheer yellow lounging pajamas.

"Oh! It's only you," she remarked disappointingly. "I was expecting to see someone else standing there in the hallway." Rea gave Vance a quick once-over look. "I see you've gotten yourself some new clothes. Ohhhhh -- and you took my advice and took a bath too! You smell a whole lot better today. Scrubbing yourself clean must have worn you out," she said sarcastically.

Vance was slowly becoming annoyed with Rea's obnoxious sense of humor. "Look, foxey lady," he began, "do you want me to stand out here in the hallway and catch cold? I'm still not dry from my bath yet. Are you going to invite me in?"

Rea stepped aside, motioning with her hand, for Vance to enter the apartment. Vance walked straight to the large couch and sat down. Rea dropped herself into a lounge chair directly across from him.

"Would you like a drink before we get down to business?" she politely asked.

"Skip the booze for now. Let's get on with the business we have to discuss. Where's the package I'm supposed to pick up from you along with the new list?" Vance was eager to get his hands on the drugs and leave the apartment as quickly as possible. He still didn't trust Rea.

Rea stood up, walked over to a closet, and removed an overnight bag from inside it.

"Everything's in here," she replied, slapping the bag with her hand, then walked to the couch. She placed the overnight bag on top of the cocktail table and sat down on the couch next to Vance. She opened the bag, removed a large manila envelope and handed it to him.

"Inside that envelope you'll find next month's list along with your fake driver's license, auto registration, and keys for the car downstairs. Did you see the car when you passed the building?"

"Yea, I looked at it," Vance removed the contents from inside the envelope and read the papers over carefully.

"The papers are all falsified. You shouldn't have any problems with them. Do you have any questions about the new list?"

"No, I understand everything perfectly."

"You know Clicker, with those new clothes, the haircut, and that fancy Van Dyke beard, you're really not a bad looking guy. Why not have that drink with me now?"

Vance put the papers back in the envelope, placed the envelope in the overnight bag, and locked it.

"O.K." he smiled. "I'll have one before I leave -- but only one!"

Rea stood and walked over to the bar. Turning, she looked at Vance. "What'll be your pleasure?"

"Make mine whiskey and water. Mix it half and half, and throw in a couple of ice cubes." Vance stood and walked over to the bar. Rea poured the drinks and handed one to him. She sat on the bar stool next to him, sipping her drink slowly.

"Rea, as long as we're going to be working together, what do you say we take off the boxing gloves and become friends?"

Rea smiled. "O.K., it's a truce." She lifted her glass and offered a toast to their new found friendship. They smiled -- then drank.

"Now that we're finally friends Rea, can I speak frankly?"

"Sure. What do you want to talk about, Clicker?" she asked coyly.

"Come on, let's go over to the couch where we can be comfortable while we chat." he suggested.

They moved from the bar to the couch, carrying their drinks. Rea set her glass down on the cocktail table, lifted her feet off of the floor, and tucked them under her butt. She placed her hands behind her head making her already large breasts -- more noticeable.

"O.K., Clicker. What's up?"

"There's still a lot of things about this organization that I don't understand. Stripes didn't get around to explaining them to me. Maybe you can clear up some of my questions?"

"For example?" she asked.

"When the radios are shipped from Brazil, how are they packed so they don't get broken? And, are they packed the same way when you ship them through the United States mail?"

Rea finished her drink and stood up. "Drink up and I'll make us a fresh one." Vance quickly finished his drink and handed her his empty glass. While she mixed the fresh drinks, she continued speaking. "The radios are shipped in special reinforced corrugated cartons from Brazil.

Cloth sacks filled with a soft substance are placed all around the radios, absorbing any blows that the cartons may encounter."

Have you got any of those sacks laying around the apartment right now?"

Rea stopped mixing the drinks. She looked suspiciously at Vance. "Why are you so interested in the packaging material? Why should you care about it?"

Vance realized he'd opened his big mouth again -- too soon. As usual, he'd been to anxious for information. Now he'd have to convince Rea it meant nothing to him. "I don't really care about the material, Rea. I'm just a stickler for the smallest of details -- that's all. When I get involved in something, I like to know about everything that makes it tick."

Rea accepted Vance's explanation and finished mixing the drinks. She walked back to the couch, carrying a tray with six drinks on it, and set it down on the cocktail table.

"Why all the extra drinks?"

"I hate to keep running back to the bar every time my glass is empty," she answered, removing two glasses from the tray. She handed one glass to Vance. "We'll be here for awhile, so I mixed an emergency supply for us. In the bottom drawer of that desk, over there," she said pointing, "you'll find a couple of bags of that packing material." Vance put his empty glass down and picked up a fresh drink off of the tray. "By the way Rea, where's Stripes at tonight? I haven't seen him for several days."

Rea moved closer to Vance's side. Several buttons on the front of her blouse had managed to work their way open. Rea's full, plump, perfectly rounded breasts exposed themselves to Vance's startled gaze. He gulped down the rest of his third drink, hoping to put out the fire that was starting in his loins. Rea moved closer to him.

"What other questions have you got?" Rea asked slyly. She placed her hand on Vance's thigh and rubbed gently, then slowly slid her hand down on his crotch. He put his empty glass down and picked up another full one off of the tray.

"Where's the drug lab located?" he asked, trying to change the subject.

Rea stopped sipping her drink. "What lab are you talking about?" I don't know anything about any lab."

Again Vance tried to change the subject, figuring that Rea was lying, or she actually knew nothing about the lab. "Skip it," he said. "I just thought Stripes had a small lab for cutting the heroin and making his dime packets."

Rea was almost sitting on Vance's lap. She removed her warm hand from Vance's crotch, and slid it inside of his shirt. She rubbed her hand slowly over his hairy chest and gently kissed his earlobe, then started blowing warm bursts of hot breath into his ear with her mouth. Vance finished another drink and picked up a fresh one.

"Clicker," she whispered softly, gently rubbing the nape of his neck with her finger tips, "haven't you got another name besides, Clicker? I hate that name."

Vance responded instantly without any hesitation, "Sure! It's Vance. Vance Marta----." He shut up before he said any more. He'd finally done it. The alcohol had done its job well. Had he blown his cover? He had to get out of that apartment before Rea began to put two and two together.

Rea stood up, bent over, and kissed Vance on his lips. Her lips were hotter than the devil's branding iron. The lounging pajamas had completely opened down the front, revealing the complete beautiful curves of her nude body.

"Wait here," she whispered into his ear, "I'll call you when I'm ready."

She went into her bedroom. Vance watched her movements in the mirror, hanging on the bedroom wall. She removed her pajamas and stood in front of the large mirror -- admiring her nude body. When she finished, she arranged herself invitingly on the bed.

It finally dawned on Vance just what Rea had on her devilish mind. If those few drinks made him tell her his real name, there was no telling what her beautiful body would make him confess. She planned on getting as much information as she possibly could out of him, and she didn't care how she went about doing it. He couldn't take a chance and stay here in the apartment with her -- not in the condition he was in.

Vance got up from the couch, walked over to the desk and removed a packet of packaging material. He put the packet into his pocket, picked up the overnight bag and left the apartment quietly, forgetting to close the desk drawer.

79

"I'm ready Vance," Rea shouted. *"You can come in now!"*

No one answered her summons. Rea stormed into the living room. One quick glimpse around the room told her that Vance had left the apartment. Looking towards the desk, the partly opened bottom drawer caught her attention. She rushed over to the desk, pulled the drawer completely out, and counted the packets inside. One of the packets was missing. Vance had to have taken it. Rea was so enraged with anger that she grabbed a bottle of whiskey off the bar and sent it crashing against the living room wall, splashing whiskey all over her nude body.

Vance took the elevator down to the first floor. He completely ignored the doorman as he walked passed him and headed straight for his car. He hated to think about what he had just passed up, but it was just one of the sacrifices that his job demanded. That is, if he wanted to stay healthy. Vance started the car's engine and headed for his hotel.

From now on, he knew he'd better double up on his guard -- whenever Rea was around...

CHAPTER 16

Vance had a hunch that these packets of packaging material had something to do with the poison found in the bad batch of heroin. His delivery schedule was short that week. He wasn't required to pick up another shipment from Rea until the following Saturday night.

He included the sample of packaging material in with his reports that he sent to Captain Reese, hoping that he'd verify his suspicions about the contents in the bag.

The following day, Vance called Captain Reese, using the special emergency telephone number. His hunch had been confirmed by the Captain. The sack contained a mixture of that special Brazilian poison, but which one was actually guilty of using the poison -- Stripes or Rea? Vance was determined to find out the answer to that question when he visited Rea on Saturday night.

The meetings with the contacts went well except for one specific Wednesday night, when Vance had encountered two problems.

He left his apartment carrying two kilos of heroin for his 8:00 p.m. appointment.

He was early. It was only 7:00 p.m. With an hour to kill before he met his contact, Vance decided to take a leisurely stroll along Klauser Street. As he approached the corner of Sixth and Klauser, he was stopped by a young man in his late twenties carrying a camera.

"Good evening," greeted the stranger, "I'm William Shell, a local reporter for the Herald newspaper. I'm writing a feature story about this area. You know, the kinds of people that live here, their jobs, their living environment -- stuff like that. Could I take a few shots and interview you? Maybe, ask you a few questions about your life here on Klauser Street?"

Vance couldn't afford to have his picture plastered on the front page of one of the largest newspapers in the city.

"Say, *scum-scriber*," he said bitterly, "get the hell away from me. I'm not interested in you or your story, and I don't want my picture in your lousy newspaper." Vance's sudden outburst took the reporter by surprise.

"What was that name you called me -- a *scum-scriber*? What's that?" asked the reporter.

"Look, all you guys are the same. All you ever do is write about people who are in some kind of trouble. If a small scandal pops up, you guys plaster it all over the front page of the newspaper. You thrive on people's miseries. That's why you're a *scum-scriber*! Now get out of my way, I've got an appointment to keep and I'm due there now."

Vance left the reporter, standing on the sidewalk, looking stunned, after the verbal attack on him.

It was 7:55 p.m. Vance arrived at the prearranged meeting place. A short, chubby man approached him at exactly 8:00 p.m. The special code words were spoken between them. Vance handed over the package containing the two kilos of heroin. The stranger handed Vance a white envelope in return for the drugs.

Vance only walked a hundred feet away from the contact when he heard someone shout -- "*Stop!*" A young policeman, walking a foot post, approached him. Vance didn't move. The office gave Vance a strange, questionable look.

"Say, don't I know you?" he asked, positive that he had seen Vance somewhere before.

"No, you don't know me," Vance answered loudly. Looking out the corner of his eye, he noticed that the contact was hiding himself in a dark doorway -- just watching and listening to see what was happening.

"Sure! I know you! You're Vance -- Vance Martall. We graduated from the Police Academy together. It's me Vance -- Jerry Westerson. Don't you remember me?" were the blurted words from the young policeman's mouth. "What in hell are you doing dressed like that?"

OH--no, thought Vance. This stupid guy forgot what he was taught about undercover work at the academy. It was pounded into our heads that when you see someone that you know, or think you know, never say anything until he makes the first move and talks to you. Vance didn't know if the contact had heard any of the conversation, but he had to stop Jerry before he went any farther with his conversation.

"Jerry, it is me -- Vance Martall," he whispered softly. "I've got to talk fast, so just keep your mouth shut and listen. We're being watched right now! I'm working undercover on a hot case. That's all I can tell you. Take out your night stick and hit me across my back. Yell at me to get out of the area and for God's sake forget that you ever saw me. Don't tell anyone!"

The young patrolman followed Vance's instructions. He took out his night stick. Yelling loudly, he swung and hit Vance across his back. Vance staggered from the blow, but regained his balance and quickly walked away.

Vance knew that news of this encounter wouldn't take long to get back to Stripes and Rea. He only hoped that his little charade had appeared convincing enough for the contact, who was still watching as Vance walked away.

Well, Saturday night would tell the whole story...

CHAPTER   17

Saturday evening had arrived. Vance was prepared for any situation that might arise. Laying across his bed, he wondered how Captain Reese's plans were shaping up. Each time Vance met a contact, the contact was arrested as soon as Vance was out of the area. Captain

Reese was handling each arrest personally. All Vance had to do was let him know when, where, and at what time to be there.

Vance had pushed a few small packets, but they were special packets that he'd personally put together. Substituting fine powdered sugar for heroin, he sold the packets for the regular street prices to the street addicts. He emphasized that this was the purest heroin they had ever gotten from Stripes. Vance kept the genuine packets of heroin hidden in his room. After his clients realized what they had gotten from him, Vance was sure that all hell would break loose when word got back to Stripes. The final showdown was coming, and Vance knew that it would be soon -- it might even be tonight.

He recounted the twenty-five envelopes he had gotten from the contacts. Each envelope had a series of letters on it. It was a special code identifying the buyer. Only Stripes could identify from whom the coded envelopes came from.

Vance dropped the envelopes into the empty overnight bag and went down to his car.

It was exactly 6:45 p.m. when he approached Stripes' apartment building. He parked his car a half block away from the entrance and watched who entered and exited the building. Vance positioned himself comfortably on the seat, lit up a cigarette, and relaxed as he watched the lights go on in Stripes' apartment. To many problems had arisen at one time for him -- really more than he thought he could handle. The bubble was getting bigger each day. Hopefully, today wasn't the day it was going to burst, but sitting in the car and worrying about it wouldn't solve anything. Vance convinced himself that he'd better get moving. Picking up the overnight bag off the car seat, he exited the car and walked towards the building -- to what might be the toughest ordeal he'd face yet.

The elevator gave a slight jolt as it stopped at the sixteenth floor. Vance stepped off and walked to the apartment doorway. Pressing the signal buzzer button, he held it in for several seconds, then released it and waited. No reply came from within the apartment. The door suddenly swung open, revealing Rea standing in the entrance way. She looked disturbed when she saw it was Vance standing in the hallway.

"I was hoping that it wasn't you," she remarked. She stepped aside to let him enter the apartment. Vance remained silent as he walked over to the couch, sat down, and placed the overnight bag down on the cocktail table. Rea shut the door, walked over to the chair opposite Vance, and sat down. No drinks were offered this time.

"Have you got this weeks load ready for me?" asked Vance, starting the conversation.

Rea folded her arms across her chest and stared at Vance -- still remaining silent. After a few moments, she finally remarked, "Cut out the fuckin' bullshit, honey! You're not getting another speck of our *Angel Dust* from us."

"What are you talking about now, Rea?" What about my deliveries for this coming week.?"

"*God-damn it! I said cut the fuckin' act!*" she screamed. "*You're not getting another fuckin' ounce of drugs from us -- you mother fuckin' lying cop!*"

It was all over, and Vance knew it, but somehow he still had to try and bluff his way out of this mess. He had to find out just how much Rea actually knew about him.

"Hey baby, are you nuts? I'm no crummy cop. Have you been sniffing to much of your own powder? It's put you out on cloud nine."

Rea stood up and walked over to the desk. She pulled open the middle drawer, removed a .38-caliber revolver from it and quickly turned around, pointing the gun at Vance.

Vance felt a lump slowly rise in his throat as he tried to swallow his fear. Unpredictable as she was, he didn't know just how far Rea would go with this escapade. He guessed that she'd fire the gun without the slightest hesitation. He had to keep on talking to her. It was his only chance for survival.

"Listen baby, what makes you so sure that I'm a cop?" Vance was stalling for time. He was waiting for that opportune moment to grab the gun away from her.

Rea motioned with the gun. "Sit up straight on that couch, and put your hands on your knees so I can keep an eye on them!"

Vance followed her instructions. She walked back to her chair and sat down, still pointing the gun directly at Vance's chest. "Since you have to be convinced that I know all about you, I'll satisfy you by telling you everything that I know. I always had a funny feeling about you, even after the first time we met. You asked too many questions about a lot of things that didn't concern you. When you came here last Saturday, I was determined to find out more about you. You made several bad mistakes.

"The first was when you took that bag of packaging material, you didn't close the desk drawer all the way. I noticed it right away when I came out of my bedroom and you were gone. The second incident was when that cop recognized you after you met your contact. Incidentally, that contact was picked up five minutes after he called me on the phone and told me what had happened. In fact, I've got proof that every contact you met was arrested in just a matter of minutes after you left that area.

"Your real name is Vance Martall. I had a friend of mine do some research for me at the public library. He checked all the back issues of the newspaper files for the past three years. And can you guess what he found? Don't try, I'll tell you. He found your name and your picture taken about a year ago in the City Council Chambers. It was a picture of some graduating cops. Want me to continue -- Officer Martall?" Rea had a small smirk on her mouth.

"No, you don't have to continue." Vance knew that the game was over for him. "What happens now that you know who I am?"

Rea threw back her head and laughed loudly, then abruptly stopped laughing. "I'm going to kill you of course -- asshole! What did you think I was going to do with you?"

Vance still had to keep stalling for more time. "I thought that we could talk this situation over. Maybe come up with some kind of a deal between us"

"Make a deal? With you? What do you take me for? Some stupid broad. As long as you're alive sweetheart, you're a threat to my life and freedom. In fact, you're the most dangerous threat to our entire organization."

"What about Stripes? I don't think he'll like you killing me without even consulting him first."

"You'll be long gone by the time Stripes gets the news about you, honey. He'll hear my side of the story, and with the evidence that I have against you, he'll be more than happy that I got rid of you."

"Well, as long as you're going to kill me, how about pacifying me and answer a few questions?" Vance tried to wipe the sweat off the palms of his hands.

"There's nothing lost in telling you what you want to know, Vance, since you'll never get a chance to repeat it to anyone -- anyway. Go ahead, ask your questions."

"Who was responsible for saturating the street with those bad drugs -- you or Stripes?"

Rea looked surprised. "You caught on to that little caper too I see. That sweet little enterprise was strictly my own idea, sweetheart. Stripes doesn't have the slightest idea what I've been doing with my own time. I'm building my own beautiful nest egg for an early retirement -- settling down in the Bahamas. With what I've got stashed away now, I can live comfortably for many years to come.

"How did you happen to run across that dangerous drug?" asked Vance.

"We originally used another type of packaging material when we shipped the radios through the mails. It didn't work out very well. So, about six months ago, Stripes came home with those new sacks of material. I was curious about them. I opened one of the sacks and was surprised to see that the material inside looked exactly like heroin. It even had the same bitter taste, so I got an idea and started mixing my own packets. I only sold them when the street supply ran low."

"Didn't you realize that you were feeding a poison to those poor unsuspecting fools who were buying your shit out there?"

"Who cares? Those assholes on the street would have eventually killed themselves with an overdose of heroin anyway. I just helped them to do it a little earlier -- that's all. Anyway, I didn't find out that the powder was a poison until a month later, when I had one of our chemists analyze the powder for me."

"You mean to say that you actually had the gall to keep circulating that stuff, even after you knew it would kill anyone who used it?" replied Vance, finding it hard to believe that any woman could be that cold hearted.

"As I said before, Vance baby -- *so what!* I'm in this for the dough, and I'm making plenty of it -- no matter who gets hurt."

Rea began to feel the weight of the gun. The gun began to waver from side to side as she tried to steady her hand.

"All right, mother fucker, stand up!" she ordered. "We've been talking about my business to long. It's about time I brought this cozy meeting to a climax. Walk over to those windows!"

"What are you going to do?" Vance asked nervously.

"Makes no difference to me, either you jump or I push you out the window, or I'll just shoot you right here. Either way, you'll wind up dead. I couldn't care less at which way you chose to die." she remarked.

86

"If I'm shot, you'll have a lot of explaining to do for the police." Suddenly it occurred to Vance that he was actually pleading for his life.

"I'll just tell them that you were an intruder. You forced your way into this apartment and tried to attack me. I managed to get to the desk and grab the gun out of the drawer. I'll convince them that I had to shoot you in self-defense. I won't have any problems, honey. Don't you worry your little ole' ass about Rea."

She stood up, motioning with the gun for Vance to walk over to the windows. "Now get up and move that fucking copper ass of yours!"

Vance felt beads of perspiration forming on his forehead. His legs felt like rubber bands. He could hardly support himself standing. He walked slowly over to the windows, stalling for time. Vance knew that his time had run out. This was actually it for him.

Rea pulled a white cord. The blue satin drapes slid to one side of the windows.

"Lift up that window," she ordered, pointing.

Vance looked at Rea, watching her finger tighten on the gun's trigger. He hesitated. The hammer on the revolver moved back slowly as her finger continued to squeeze. Vance lifted the window slowly upward with both hands -- just as Rea had ordered.

"Now sit on the outside ledge with your legs hanging out!"

Vance obeyed. He hung one leg over the ledge, then turned towards Rea. He realized at that moment he was staring death in the face. Often in the past, he had wondered just how he would feel when his time came. Now, with just minutes away, he would actually find out.

"For God's sake, Rea," he pleaded, "don't do this to me. We're sixteen floors up -- not this way!"

"*I told you to sit on that window ledge,*" Rea shouted angrily. She pulled the hammer on the gun all the way back with her thumb. Vance turned around slowly, preparing to put his other leg out on the window ledge.

Rea walked towards Vance, ready to help him go out the window as soon as he lifted his other leg over the ledge.

The front door suddenly swung open, making a loud *thud* noise against the wall. Stripes stood in the doorway carrying a black leather attaché case. The expression on his face was one of confusion. He tried to analyze the scene taking place before his eyes.

"*Just what in the hell is going on?*" he screamed. Stripes walked into the apartment and slammed the entrance door shut behind him. "Will one of you two idiots please tell me what's going on for Christ sake!"

Vance quickly turned and slid himself off the window ledge. Rea stepped backwards, surprised by Stripes entrance into the apartment. Vance was sure that Stripes would believe Rea's story as soon as he heard it from her, but he still had to try and bluff his way out. Either way, he knew that the odds were against him.

"Stripes," Rea began speaking excitedly, "I've got a beaut of a story to tell you. You'd better sit down and have a drink first." She still pointed her gun at Vance.

"I'll stand," replied Stripes, "just get on with your story."

"Our friend here is actually working for the police department. How's that for a fuckin' good swift kick in the ass?"

Stripes looked at Vance, disbelieving what he had just heard. "Is that true, Clicker? Are you working for the cops?"

"He's a cop all right," interrupted Rea, "and his real name is Vance Martall -- Officer Vance Martall."

"Shut up." Stripes was both angry and upset at the thought of him making a bad mistake in choosing and thrusting his new confidant. "Let him tell me himself, Rea. I want to hear from his own lips that he's a cop."

Here was Vance's chance. He could see that Stripes was angry with Rea's statement. Could he get Stripes to believe him instead of her -- he wondered?

"Sure I worked with the cops," said Vance. "As a matter of fact, you told me too."

"What are you talking about, Clicker?" Stripes was surprised with Vance's statement.

"She's talking about the time I helped out the cops by giving them the information on that pawn shop fence. I just told the cops what you wanted me too. And now that we're letting the cats out of the bag, here's a few little tid bits that I found out about your precious little princess here. Did you know that she's been double-crossing you?" Stripes stared at Rea. His eyes filled with disbelief.

"Don't believe a word he's saying, honey." Rea interrupted Vance. "He had all of our contacts arrested this week after he delivered the drugs to them."

"Are you telling me that he didn't bring any money with him when he came here tonight?"

"Sure I did." Vance quickly walked over to the cocktail table. He opened the overnight bag and dumped all the envelopes on the couch. "Check those envelopes out and see if everything's on the up and up." Rea was still holding the gun towards him.

Stripes carefully examined the fronts of all the envelopes. He tore one open and counted the money inside of it. "Everything checks out, Rea. It's all here. How do you explain that? If he was a cop he wouldn't have brought all of this dough here -- would he sweetheart?"

Vance spoke again before Rea could open her mouth. "This little doll of yours, Stripes, has really a neat little operation going for herself. Sure the contacts were arrested, but do you want to really know why? Well, I'll tell you why. She tipped off the cops anonymously by mail. With all of the contacts under arrest and all of your drugs off of the streets, she had a chance to push her own shit."

"Her shit? What the hell are you talking about Clicker?"

Vance walked over to the desk, opened the bottom drawer and removed a sack of packaging material. He tore open the sack and spilled the contents on top of the desk.

"Take a look at that. She's been mixing that crap with heroin and making her own small packets. With all of your drugs off the streets, she was free to operate and charge any amount that she wanted for her packets. Here's another beautiful bit of information that you might interest you. This packaging material is made from a Brazilian plant that kills anyone who injects it into their blood stream. She's been passing that stuff on the streets as part of your drugs. She has a sizable amount of dough stashed away, figuring on an early retirement for herself."

"Aaron, don't listen to------."

"Rea baby," Stripes interrupted her, "my name's Stripes -- remember?"

"You've got to listen to me," Rea screamed, almost in tears. *"He's lying! Can't you see that he's lying?"*

"Sure, baby, sure." Stripes took the gun out of her hand.

Rea was close to the point of total hysteria when she realized that Stripes was siding with Vance. She started to run for the front door hoping to get away from them. Stripes pole-vaulted over the couch and tackled her by the ankles -- bringing her down to the floor.

Before she had a chance to scream, Stripes stuffed his handkerchief in her mouth while Vance held her hands behind her back.

"What are you going to do with her?"

"Don't worry about her, Clicker. I'll take care of her by myself. Rea and I understand each other. Don't we baby?"

Rea's eyes filled with tears as the look of fear emerged on her face. She tried desperately to break away from her captors.

"Hit her in the jaw Stripes and knock her out."

"Never mind. You just do what I tell you to do. Go over to the bar and get me a fresh bottle of the bonded bourbon." Stripes removed the belt from his pants and tied Rea's hands securely behind her back. He leaned on Rea to keep her down. Vance came back with the bottle of whiskey.

"Hold onto her for a minute." Stripes went into the bedroom, pulled a bed sheet off of the bed and tore it into long thin strips. They used the strips of cloth to tie Rea's legs together. Vance rolled Rea over on her back. Stripes knelt down and picked up the bottle of whiskey.

"Clicker, listen to me. I want you to remove the handkerchief from her mouth when I tell you to--O.K.? -- *Do it now!*"

Vance quickly removed the cloth from Rea's mouth. Stripes immediately shoved the neck of the opened whiskey bottle into it. "Hold her head still." Stripes pinched Rea's nostrils with his right thumb and index finger, forcing her to gulp down large swallows of whiskey, as she tried to breathe through her mouth.

"A few minutes of this and she'll be out cold, then we won't have to worry about her for awhile."

Rea struggled, choked, and gagged as she tried desperately to push the neck of the bottle out of her mouth, using her tongue. It was useless. She finally fainted.

"What are you going to do with her now?"

"I don't really know," said Stripes. "I'll have to think about it for awhile. Maybe I'll simmer down later on and have a good long talk with her. Everything depends on her attitude. In the meantime, I want you to get the hell out of here."

"What about this weeks deliveries ,Stripes?"

"I'll get in touch with you tomorrow and we'll talk about it then. In the meantime, you go home and just wait there until you hear from me."

"Are you sure you can handle everything by yourself?" asked Vance, hesitant about leaving.

"Yea--sure--just go!" Stripes was losing his patience.

Vance was concerned about Stripes' state of mind, but he had to think of his own skin. He figured that Rea would be all right -- maybe after a little beating and a couple of broken arms. It would serve her right for what she wanted to do to him.

Vance took the elevator down to the main floor, left the building, and started walking towards his car. As he crossed the street, two women walking towards him, from the opposite direction, looked upward and screamed. Vance turned around and looked up, just in time to see a dark figure falling crazily through the air from one of the top floors in Stripes' building.

The figure hit the ground with a loud *thud* and just laid there -- motionless. Vance ran over to see who it was. Deep within, he guessed who it would be -- and his guess was right. It was Rea. Her broken body laid still and limp on the blood spattered sidewalk.

Vance walked back to his car and vomited at the curb. When he finished throwing up his guts, he sat down in the driver's seat. He lit a cigarette, trying to steady his shaking hand, then started the car and looked up at Stripes' apartment. He watched the window drapes close and the lights go out. He knew how the coroner's report would read -- accidental death due to falling out of a window while being intoxicated! This was just one more score he had to settle with Stripes.

Driving off, he looked for the first open bar that he could find, so he could get good and drunk. He had to try to forget this nightmare that he'd just witnessed. Just for awhile, he wanted to forget what Stripes would do to him if he ever suspected who Vance really was, and that Rea was right about him all the time.

Now he'd have to be twice as careful about his identity than he had been before...

CHAPTER 18

The loud pounding on the door sounded like a hundred cannons exploding at one time inside of Vance's head. He got good and drunk the night before, but it really hadn't served any good purpose except to give him a bigger headache. His problems still existed. Nothing had really changed for him.

The pounding on the door continued. Vance's temples ached with a throbbing sensation that seemed to keep time with the beating on the door.

"*Who the hell is it?*" Vance shouted, holding the sides of his head with both hands.

"Come on, old buddy, open up," came a reply from the other side of the door," it's me -- Stripes."

Vance lifted himself off the bed and walked to the door, being very careful not to jar his aching head. He turned the key, opened the door slowly, and was greeted by Stripes standing out in the hallway with a great big smile on his face. Stripes walked into the room, ignoring Vance standing in the doorway.

"Hurry up and get dressed, we've got a busy day ahead of us."

Vance ran his fingers through the front of his hair, pushing the long strands back away from his eyes. "What time is it?" he asked, angry at Stripes for waking him up.

"It's a quarter past twelve in the afternoon." Stripes laughed. "Boy, from the looks of you, you really hung a good one on last night."

"Yea, well, you know how it is. Once in awhile a guy has to get good drunk to rid his mind of things that he just wants to forget."

"Say, what's bugging you Clicker? Is it that scene with Rea last night? If it is, don't worry about her. I took care of that problem right after you left."

"Yea, I know. I saw how you remedied that problem! I saw her fall. What the hell did you have to kill her for?"

"Kill her?" Stripes acted surprised. "I never touched her. She accidentally fell out of the open window."

"Yea, I understand Stripes -- no witnesses. That's why you had me leave the apartment so quickly. Couldn't you have worked her over enough to convince her that she should come around to your way of thinking?"

"Don't worry about it." Stripes smiled, slapping his hand on Vance's shoulder. "There's no loose ends to worry about now. I made sure of that. You're not connected in any way with her death. Here, read this." Stripes reached into his back pocket and pulled out the morning newspaper. He pointed to a small news clip item printed on the bottom of page three. The item stated that while in a state of severe intoxication, Rea had lost her balance and had fallen out of the window when she opened it to get some fresh air.

Vance crumpled the newspaper with his hands and threw it on the bed. He gave Stripes a fed up look. "Yea, I read the article, only you and I know better -- don't we?"

Stripes ignored Vance's concern over Rea's death. He assumed that in time, Vance would forget all about it -- just as he would. "Come on and get dressed, we've got to get going."

"*God-damn it! Will you quite rushing me,*" Vance shouted angrily. "*I haven't even taken a piss yet.*"

"O.K.-- O.K." Stripes sat down on a wooden chair. He tried to calm Vance. "Go and take your piss -- take your sweet time too. I'll wait."

Vance walked over to the small sink, turned on the cold water faucet, and stuck his head under the tap. His head was quickly numbed by the ice cold water that fell on it. Vance grabbed a paper towel and left the room without uttering another word, heading directly for the bathroom. He returned to his room a short while later, feeling a little better after he had relieved himself. He was still not in full control of all his mental and physical faculties. As soon as he entered the room he threw a few quick questions at Stripes.

"All right, what happens now? How do we make the deliveries? Who's going to make up the lists and get them to the customers?"

"That's why I'm here now, Clicker. A long time ago I figured that this list system wouldn't last forever. So, while I was away these few months, I was setting up a whole new operation. It's too bad Rea didn't play it straight with me. She would have liked the new set-up. She would have made twice the amount of dough then she made when she was selling on her own. Well, that's all water under the bridge. Get the keys for the car and let's get going."

"Where are we going?" asked Vance, picking up the car keys off the table and tucking them into his pant's pocket.

"We're going over to the other side of town," replied Stripes as he walked out of the room.

The drive, to the other end of the city, seemed to take forever. Stripes talked without really saying anything worth while. Occasionally he commented on a girl's figure as they drove passed her. Vance ignored most of the conversation. He was thinking about the report he would write for Captain Reese that night.

Vance continued driving, always following Stripes directions, occasionally making a right turn and then a left -- always making a mental note of the streets that he drove on. The overcast sky began releasing a fine wet mist that quickly covered the windshield. Vance turned on the windshield wipers. The movement of the wiper blades seemed to have a hypnotic effect on both of them.

Stripes repositioned himself on the car seat and folded his arms across his chest. Smiling, he looked at Vance. "Clicker, I've decided to bring you in as a full partner. Hummm....with a small salary of course, until that forty grand you owe me is paid back in full. Now that Rea's gone, I've got to have somebody next to me I can really trust. I know that you're definitely that person."

Vance forced a smile of approval. "Sounds great to me boss -- really great!" he managed to blurt out.

They were now approaching the older section of the city. Most of the homes were shabby and weather beaten.

"Turn right at that intersection," ordered Stripes. He sat up erect. Vance followed the instructions and made a sharp right turn at the intersection. They traveled a few hundred feet along a dark street. "Park the car in front of that gray two-story house ,just up ahead of us, on the right," said Stripes.

Vance brought the car to a complete stop in front of the designated house. He gave the surrounding area a quick once-over as Stripes got out of the car. The tall, gray house stood in the middle if the block on a large lot. The neighboring house on the right hinted of being occupied by the lights glowing in a few of the windows. The house on the opposite side had broken windows and blistering paint on its' wooden frame. Vance figured that the house had been abandoned for quite some time. People walking passed the car were totally disinterested in the strangers who were entering their secluded neighborhood.

Vance got out of the car and walked along side of Stripes. They walked up the narrow sidewalk leading to the house. Vance looked for a house number, but none was visible.

"Whose place is this?"

"Mine," replied Stripes. "I bought it about three months ago."

"What in the hell would you want with this firetrap?" said Vance laughing. "This house is at least one hundred years old."

"Ninety six years old to be exact." Stripes corrected Vance. He became very serious. "I bought this place specifically for its' age and the neighborhood. For what I intend to use it for, it fits my needs perfectly."

Stripes removed a set of keys from his pant's pocket. He carefully selected a key and used it to open the entrance door.

"Come on in Clicker, but be careful where you step until I find that damn light switch."

Stripes finally located the light switch and turned it on. Large corrugated cartons, stacked one on top of the other, filled the entire living room of the first floor apartment. The sight of all the cartons confused Vance. Each carton bore the name of a different pharmaceutical supply house along with the quantity and kind of merchandise inside of each carton.

"Where in hell did you gather all those cartons from? asked Vance, looking puzzled. "What are you going to do with all this stuff? Did you go to those factories and buy that merchandise yourself?"

"No." Stripes walked over to one of the cartons and opened it. "Give me credit for having some brains, Clicker. All these cartons were picked up within the last three months. This is all hot merchandise that I've bought from the local kids. They stole it. I spread the word around on what I wanted and managed to get everything I asked for. These cartons were stolen from the backs of trucks, stores, and from the factories themselves.

" I bought each carton from a different person. I also picked up each shipment at a different location. I brought these cartons here very late at night, when I was sure that everyone in the neighborhood was asleep. No one will know what we're doing here in the house. And, none of these cartons can be traced back to me or this house."

"Another question Stripes."

"What is it Clicker?"

"You said *we'll* be doing something here -- who's we?"

"First, a little more explanation is needed here, Clicker. This house is going to be my new base of operations. I'm moving you out of that rat's nest you live in and putting you up right here. You and I are the only ones who are going to know about this place and operate my machinery."

"Machinery? What kind of machinery are you talking about? Hey, I ain't no kind of a mechanic you know."

"It's all downstairs in the basement. I'll show it all to you later."

"The idea of me living here sounds all right to me Stripes, but where'll you be staying?"

"I'll continue living in my apartment. I've got to leave town again for a week or so. I've got a few more deals brewing in the pot. There are a lot of loose ends that I have to take care of, but when I'm finished we'll have a real sweet set-up going for the both of us, but first, we've got a lot of work ahead of us. I've got a lot of teaching to do, and you've got a lot to learn before this night is over."

Vance was still confused. "If I live here, Stripes, where will I park the car? If the neighbors should ask questions, who do I tell them I am?"

"I'm taking the car with me tonight, Clicker. I want you here in the house for the next week or so. I don't want you to leave this place for any reason at all! If by some slim chance, someone should see you, tell them you and your brother just moved into the house and that your brother's a salesman who's out of town right now."

"What about all of my clothes and personal stuff back at the hotel room? I'm not going to leave anything behind again. What about food for me?"

"You have an ample supply of canned goods in the kitchen to last you through the month. I'll pick up your clothes when I leave here. You've got your camera with you already. You shouldn't have to much more back there."

Vance had to do some fast thinking. He had to be the one who went back to his hotel room and gathered all the writing materials. He couldn't take a chance on Stripes find them. Then there was the problem of all those packets of heroin he had hidden behind the dresser. He had to get them to Captain Reese -- somehow.

"Listen Stripes, I've gone along with you on everything you've asked of me ever since we met -- right?" Stripes nodded his head in agreement. "Well, I've got to go back to my place myself. I've got things put away in secret hiding places. You know, money, my best photos, stuff like that. I'd also like to leave a note at the hotel clerk's desk, so she won't call the police and report me missing. That clerk, she gets a little kooky at times and I wouldn't put it past her to pull something crazy like that. If you want me to go along with you on this deal, then you'll have to let me pick up my own things."

"All right, tell you what I have in mind. Take the car and do what you have to do. Pick up your things, but I want you back here within three hours -- at the very most."

"What about that machinery you were telling me about?"

"Never mind about that now, just get going." Stripes gave Vance directions to find his way back to the house. Vance finally left. Stripes stayed behind.

The drive back to Vance's hotel took longer than he had expected. For some unknown reason, traffic had become unusually heavy for that time of day.

Vance quickly gathered his belongings and set them on a table. It was getting late and he didn't have time to fill out a full report for Captain Reese. He quickly jotted down a few dozen lines on a piece of paper: the new place where he was living and the circumstances leading to Rea's death. He also wrote that he couldn't keep in constant touch with the Captain, but as soon as he got settled, he'd write a more detailed report.

Vance stuffed the packets of heroin into four large envelopes, addressing them to Captain Reese, care of City Hall, room 105. He scribbled a note for the hotel clerk explaining that he was moving out and going back to Ohio. He gathered his clothes, threw them into his fiberboard suitcase, and headed down the hotel's stairway. Folding the note in half, he shoved it into his room number's box on the wall behind the counter. The hotel clerk was nowhere to be found.

On the way back to Stripe's house, Vance found an outside telephone on a corner and tried to call Captain Reese, using the special telephone number. He struck out. No one answered the telephone at Captain Reese's home. All he could do now was put the envelopes, containing the notes and heroin, into four different mail boxes. He had to search different locations for the mail boxes and hurry back before Stripes started wondering what was taking him so long.

CHAPTER 19

It was a little more than three hours when Vance arrived back at the drug house. He checked the lamppost on the corner for the street's name, but the sign had been ripped off. It seemed as though this lonely street was like a tiny little island, lost in this big city.

Vance knocked on the door and waited. The door opened almost immediately.

"Did you get everything?"

"Yep, I picked up all my things and left a note for the hotel clerk."

"Great! After working on this new set-up for a couple of months, you'll be living in an apartment just like mine. Oh, before I forget, give me the keys for the car."

Vance set his suitcase down on the floor and handed Stripes the car keys. Large plastic containers, taken from several opened cartons, laid on top of a make shift table.

"Now that I'm back, let's get down to the nitty-gritty of things. Just what part do I play in this new operation of yours? What about this machinery you were talking about?"

Stripes removed a cloth bound notebook from his attaché case, set it down on top of the table, and opened it. He removed the plastic cap from one of the containers and poured some of the contents into the palm of his hand.

"Know what these are, Clicker?" he asked, holding his hand outstretched towards Vance.

"Sure. They're called *Bennies*. What about them?"

"From now on we're in the pill distribution business."

"What? You've got to be kidding. In order to make big bucks, you'd have to be pushing that stuff around the clock."

"That's the beautiful point of this operation Clicker, we don't have to personally deal with the street tripe. I've made arrangements to get rid of all this stuff out of town. It'll be shipped to almost forty-eight states. I made some deals with some big shots from other organizations. We supply the pills and package them ourselves. They'll pay us direct, so we won't have to deal with any one on the street. It'll be the biggest operation you've ever seen."

"When do we have to start shipping the pills?"

"We have a week before the first mailing list arrives, that's why we have to hurry. Each mailing carton will contain just so many packets. The people from the other organizations are going to peddle whole cartons of drugs. We'll ship the cartons to them by way of truck freight delivery. You'll pack a half dozen pills per packet. We make a *Fin* for each packet. I figure that a carton eight inches, by four inches by, four inches should hold about five hundred packets."

"Wow!" exclaimed Vance, "that's really gonna run into some pretty good dough for us." This was more valuable information that Vance had to get to Captain Reese as soon as possible. If this idea of Stripes spread nation wide, it could really prove to be disastrous.

Stripes dropped the pills back into the plastic container and twisted the cap on tight.

"Follow me Clicker. Now I'll show you the most beautiful part about this whole set-up."

They both walked down a long flight of stairs leading to the basement of the building. Stripes turned on the light switch. Bundles of unconstructed mailing cartons lined one complete wall of the basement. A wooden table stood in one corner of the room. On top of it stood several large glass bottles, each containing a clear liquid. Unmarked sealed cartons lined the entire opposite wall.

In the center of the basement floor stood a large furnace with its' metal heat ducts reaching out in every direction, like the arms of a giant octopus. Next to the furnace stood a conglomeration of metal parts that Vance had never seen before.

"What are those bundles over there?"

"Those are the cartons you'll be mailing out with the packets of pills inside, Clicker. You can either work upstairs or down here, whichever place you prefer, but that's only when you're working on packaging the pills."

Stripes pointed to the sealed unmarked cartons stacked along the opposite wall. "Those cartons contain empty plastic bottles, bottle caps, labels, staples, envelopes and a lot of other materials that you'll need for shipping the pills. There is also ten cases of sugar cubes."

"Sugar cubes?"

Stripes walked over to the table with the glass bottles on it that had clear liquid inside. "These bottles," he began, "contain a chemical called *LSD*. My two young scientific associates made this batch up for me at our lab. They're really very talented. To go on, one of your tasks will be to connect a rubber cap, with a long hose attached, over the neck of one of these bottles. At the opposite end of the hose is an attachment, that'll regulate the flow of liquid from the bottle onto the sugar cubes. You'll catch on quick enough after I show you how it's done. We'll also make a wad of dough from these sugar cubes soaked with that *LSD* chemical."

"What are you going to do with that pile of metal junk next to the furnace?" asked Vance."

"Oh, that's the prize package I was telling you about. Those are the parts for my big machinery project."

Vance examined the maze of pipes, tubing, gear boxes, and other confusing parts. He tried to connect several of the pieces. Stripes walked over to Vance. "I picked that machine up in a second hand junk shop. That place had a yard full of every type of gadget that you might be looking for."

"Can I ask you what this crap is and what's it used for?"

"It's a machine that's going to help me to manufacture my own pills. I'm going to mix my own formula and solidify the pills myself. I can cut down on the drug portion in the formula and add an equal amount of powdered sugar. That way, we cut down our operating costs and add that much more to our profits!"

"It still looks like nothing but a pile of junk to me, Stripes. Just look at it. It's rusted, dented, and out dated. This contraption will never work. Did you see it operate before you bought it?"

"Well," Stripes hesitated, "I'll admit that it's old, eighty-six years old to be exact, but it has had years of great performance behind its' credits. It's a thing of beauty and the shop owner guaranteed that it will perform to my expectations. Clicker, this was one of the first machines used in the drug industry to make pills automatically. Why, it'll produce thirty pills per minute."

"How does it operate?"

"It works on combustion."

"It reminds me of a home made still," laughed Vance.

"You're have way right, Clicker. It operates on almost the same principle as the still. Just remember one thing that's very important, never let the dials on these pressure gauges read more than three hundred and fifty degrees! If the dials go any higher than that, you'll

100

blow up the house and your ass with it. So, that's about it for down here. Let's go upstairs. I've a lot to explain to you about the formulas."

Back in the living room, Stripes referred to his notebook again. He explained the formula mixtures to Vance. When he finished, they took a tour of the rest of the house. Vance's sleeping quarters were on the second floor of the building. After Stripes showed Vance the last room in the house, the kitchen, he left.

Vance couldn't let those pills be shipped all around the country. He just couldn't let them go. Somehow -- someway -- he just had to find a solution to his problem. He only had a week to come up with a fool proof plan.

He didn't dare leave the house and try to get in touch with Captain Reese. The house might be watched, or Stripes might come back and find him gone. In either case, this time he was on his own. There'd be no Captain Reese, or the police, to come to his rescue...

CHAPTER 20

Vance followed all of Stripes instructions -- right down to the last detail. The following morning, Stripes arrived back at the house bright and early. He had two men with him. Stripes went upstairs and woke Vance up. They came down to the first floor where Stripes introduced the two men as helpers from the junk yard.

The four men went down to the basement and started the reconstruction of the pill producing machine. The two men were well acquainted with putting the parts where they belonged. Stripes explained to the two workers that the machine was going to be used to make a new type of candy pill for the kids. He was using this house because he had a secret formula that would revolutionize the candy industry, and he didn't want anyone stealing it. That's why there was all of this secrecy.

The four of them worked straight through the day until 11:30 p.m. The machine was operational with only a few problems that were soon corrected. When Stripes was satisfied with the machine's operation, he thanked the men and paid them what he promised, plus a bonus for getting the machine operational in a short amount of time. The three men shook hands with Vance and then left the house.

In the three days that followed, Vance made the diluted pills with the help of the outdated pill machine. Carefully packaging the pills in groups of six, he stapled the small envelopes closed and inserted them into the mailing cartons.

He had to do the packaging in case Stripes dropped in unexpectedly to check on his progress. He had to show some kind of production for the time he was spending there. At meal time, Vance would look out the front window and watch the neighbors walk passed the house.

One particular young girl had caught his attention the very first time that he saw her walking passed the house. For some unknown reason, her facial structure resembled the face of his little sister that had been lost in the flood waters, those many long years ago.

If she had lived, thought Vance, she probably might have looked exactly like this particular girl. When she walked, she seemed to float with each step that she took. From her actions, Vance imagined that she loved life and enjoyed living every minute of it. She was always with a group of people -- never alone.

Long straggly hair, unshaven faces, beards, shabby clothes and a complete unawareness of the entire world around them, seemed to characterize the local neighborhood people.

Vance watched the young girl and her friends enter the dilapidated house directly across the street. The shadows of night helped to blot out the potholes in the street, as well as the deep crevices in the sidewalks.

Enough daydreaming, thought Vance as he stood up from his makeshift corrugated chair. He returned to his job -- packaging the pills. Several hours passed. The sounds of happy, laughing voices and wild rhythmic music, seeped through the small opening in the window that Vance had used for ventilation.

The sounds drew his attention. He was bored and tired of packaging the pills. What he needed was a change of pace. Vance decided to light the boilers and run the compressing machine in the basement.

The arrows on the safety gauges registered just below two hundred and fifty degrees when the machinery was in full operation. Suddenly, the silence of the night was broken by a shrill, bloodcurdling scream. Vance quickly ran up the basement stairs and out into the street to investigate.

The young girl he had taken a special interest in stood on the roof of a car. In her hands she carelessly waved a revolver. A curly headed young boy stood on the sidewalk in front of her, pleading with her to give him the gun and get off the roof of the car. The girl stared at him blankly, not really seeing him standing there in front of her. She screamed violently each time he spoke to her.

Vance ran over to the young boy and offered his help. "What's wrong with her?" He grabbed the boy's arm.

"I don't know, man," replied the boy, puzzled and confused. "We were having a little party time upstairs in our apartment. You know, smoking a little grass, popping a few pills, stuff like that. One of the guys brought some acid with him -- sugar cubes saturated with *LSD*. Effie, that's her name, took one of the cubes and sucked on it till it desolved. She was all right for about ten minutes, then all hell broke loose. She made a mad dash for the window and tried to jump out of it. She kept screaming something about seeing God waiting for her on the other side of the window. I managed to pull her back into the room, but I lost my grip on her. She broke away, grabbed the gun from off the top of a dresser, and ran out here."

"Is the gun loaded?" Vance hoped that the answer was no.

"I don't know, man. It's been laying on that dresser for weeks and nobody ever touched it before now. If you ask me, she's on one hell-of-a-bad trip. A real bummer!"

Vance tried to attract the girl's attention. "Hey kid, come on down so we can have a talk. We've got a few things to discuss."

The girl stared blankly at Vance, not really seeing him standing there. Mumbling incoherent phrases, she swayed back and forth unsteadily.

"*Stay away from me,*" she screamed. "*I know who you really are. Those clothes don't fool me a bit. I see those horns on the top of your head and that pointed tail behind you. You're not going to get me. Just stay the fuck away from me.*"

"Listen kid," pleaded Vance, "give me that gun. Come on down and everything will be all right. Let's talk about it. Let me help you!"

"*I told you to stay away from me, and keep that helper of yours away from me too.*"

103

Vance lunged forward, trying to take the girl by surprise. Quickly sidestepping Vance's attempt to grab her, she stepped back and shouted, "*I warned you to stay away from me.*" She inserted the gun barrel into her mouth and squeezed the trigger. The loud explosion echoed through the night air as bits of bone fragments, brains, and blood decorated the surroundings around her. The girl's body spun around, then fell forward on top of Vance. Her blood felt warm and sticky as it flowed down his forearm. Vance lowered her body gently on the ground. After sliding her eyelids closed, Vance stood up and tried to wipe her blood off of his hands. Watching faces in the crowd displayed masks of horror and disbelief.

Vance quickly walked away from the tragic scene. A young life had been wasted for nothing more than a false thrill, caused by the greed of a bloodsucker who wanted to make a buck and didn't care how he did it.

There was nothing more he could do to help her. His eye caught the dark silhouette outline of the tall gray house across the street. Inside of that house he was manufacturing the same kind of poison that had helped to kill the girl.

Vance thought a moment and the answer came to him in a flash. He knew what had to be done before anymore of that poison got into circulation.

He ran across the street, entered the gray house and ran down the basement stairs. Vance turned the machinery controls up to the maximum output. The small arrows on the safety gauges began slowly climbing towards the red danger zone on the dials.

Vance felt exhilarated. Maybe, he thought, the explosion of the boilers wouldn't be enough force to destroy everything that had to be destroyed. Everything had to go. He searched every corner of the basement. He located partly filled paint cans and two gallons of paint thinner. He quickly emptied the contents of the paint cans into the center of the basement floor.

The safety valves on top of the boilers began whistling from the mounting pressure. This was the warning sign, that in a short amount of time, the boilers were going to blow up. The pitch got higher and higher. Vance picked up the two gallon cans of paint thinner and rushed up the basement stairs. Reaching the top step, he dumped the contents from one of the cans on the stairs, letting the clear liquid run freely down the steps. The second can was splashed on the kitchen floor and over the cartons in the living room.

Vance was half way down the narrow sidewalk, in the front of the house, when the boilers finally blew. The fierce blast sent out a shock wave that lifted him off the ground, sending him crashing into the base of a large oak tree. Stunned, but not completely unconscious, Vance watched the roof of the old gray house being slowly consumed by smoke and gulping flames. Within minutes, the entire house was engulfed in one big ball of fire. Vance had succeeded in destroying the entire shipment of narcotics -- this time without the help of Captain Reese.

Vance painfully lifted himself off of the ground and started to leave the area. The sound of wailing sirens could be heard in the distance. Reaching the corner of the block, Vance stopped to watch the fire engines stop in front of the burning inferno. He turned and started walking, not really knowing in what direction he was headed. A car screeched to a stop next to him. Vance heard Stripes' voice shout at him from inside of the car. "*Get in!*"

He obeyed without hesitation. Opening the door of the car, Vance slowly crawled in and sat down. Stripes drove off -- remaining silent. They had only driven a few blocks when Stripes slowed down the car and parked.

"All right! Explain! Just what in the hell happened back there?"

Vance found it very hard to think clearly. His head ached unmercifully, from the blow he'd sustained, when he hit his head against the tree.

"I don't know what happened, Stripes? The fuckin' boilers blew! I turned them on to make more pills. After a few minutes the safety valves started whistling like crazy. The arrows on the gauges went wild. I tried to shut the gas off, but the valve broke when I applied pressure to turn it off. All hell broke loose. Everything just went crazy. I got out of the house as fast as I could. There was nothing that I could have done to stop it. When I ran out the front door, the boilers blew. The blast picked me up and threw me against a tree. I hit my head on the fuckin' tree and split it open.

Stripes handed Vance a clean handkerchief. "Here, wipe the blood off of your face. You look like hell."

"What do we do now?"

"I'll put you up at my apartment for the time being."

Vance was surprised that Stripes was taking everything so calmly, but he was sure that a storm was soon to come.

They drove along together in silence. Vance finally began the conversation. "Boy, that house really went up in flames fast. What do we do now that the pills are gone?"

"I'll tell you one thing, Clicker, we're in trouble. And I mean -- big trouble! Here we are with a big cash down payment on all of that merchandise, and we can't ship one damn single item. I've got to do some fast talking with the clients to be a little patient for a couple of weeks. Maybe we can survive that way."

"What are you saying, Stripes? You've got more drugs stashed away somewhere else?"

"No, we're heading for my lab now. I'm going to have those two young chemists whip me up another batch of *LSD*. In a couple of days we should have enough cubes ready to be shipped."

This was it. What Vance had been working towards for the past year. Once he learned the location of Stripes' laboratory, he could pass the information on to Captain Reese and then fade out gracefully into the sunset. It would be Captain Reese's headache from then on. Just a couple more hours and everything would be over...

CHAPTER 21

Vance carefully noted their traveling directions as Stripes drove to his laboratory. They were entering a section of the city that housed a multitude of abandoned warehouses.

Stripes stopped the car in front of an old warehouse storage building bearing the name, *SEAN'S ELECTRICAL EQUIPMENT,* over the doorway.

"Is this it?" asked Vance, trying to remember the route they had taken.

"Yep. Come on in with me." Stripes got out of the car. Vance followed, quickly viewing the area for an alternate entry into the large warehouse. Stripes removed some keys from his pant's pocket, selected one, and unlocked a door.

They entered the cold, damp warehouse. Stripes closed the door behind them, locking it securely. He turned on a light switch and illuminated the entire dusty, musty smelling, rodent infested, storage area. Long strands of cobwebs hung from the exposed wooden rafters.

"Do you own this place too?"

"Sure do! Believe it or not, I picked this place up in a perfectly legal business transaction about a year ago."

"What's in all those corrugated cartons?"

"Nothing. They're empty except for some torn up cellulose. I have them there for appearance sake only, in case anyone wanders in here by mistake. A partly filled warehouse looks better than an empty one -- even if the cartons are empty."

Vance rubbed his hand over the top of one of the cartons, disrupting the dust with his finger tips. "This place is a real mess. It hasn't been used much -- has it?"

"No, not this portion of the building. Follow me, Clicker."

Vance followed Stripes up a flight of creaky old stairs. He noticed a half-dozen fifty gallon metal drums under the staircase.

"What's in those metal drums, Stripes?"

"They're suppose to be filled with some kind of cleaning fluid. They were here when I got this place. I just left them there and never bothered with them."

The stairway led to a large office on the second floor of the warehouse. The area was well illuminated by several overhead lights. Two young men sat at a long wooden table. Various sizes and shapes of glass bottles and vials were completely or partially filled with different colored fluids. The men stopped working when they saw Vance and Stripes. They quickly covered the top of the long table with a cloth, trying to hide what they were working on.

"How's everything going?" Stripes shook hands with the two men.

"Everything's going along just fine," answered one on the chemists. "We've made tremendous progress since we saw you four weeks ago."

"Yea? O.K., give me some details on just what you two have accomplished."

The two chemists hesitated, looking at Vance.

"Don't worry about him, he's all right. He's one of us. Clicker, this is....." Before Stripes could continue he was interrupted by one of the chemists.

"Stripes, never mind about our names. For the time being, let's just say that I'm Doctor Jeckel and my partner is Mister Hyde. Names are really unimportant. It's the person's personality and brains that really counts."

Stripes smiled and nodded his agreement. Vance just watched. Stripes walked over to the long table and removed the cloth covering the chemist's experiments. In the center of the table laid a pair of thin rubber surgical gloves, a small bottle of oil, an oblong metal container holding long thin strips made of an elastic substance, and several pairs of metal tweezers. There was also a small bottle of clear liquid, a large magnifying glass mounted on a metal stand, and a large stack of *Wanted* posters printed by the Federal Government.

"Would one of you explain to Clicker just what we're trying to do and just how far we've gotten on this project?"

The young chemist who had been doing all of the talking said, "In order for me to give you a full explanation of what we're trying to achieve, I'll have to start at the very beginning. Do you know anything about fingerprint identification?"

"No," Vance replied, shaking his head from side to side.

"If you had taken biology in high school, you would be familiar with the breakdown of the human skin. The patterns and special ridge characteristics that develop on our fingers, hands, and feet begin to take form four to five months before we are actually born. Nature supplied us with this frictional skin so we could hold on to objects and not slip when walking on a smooth wet surface.

"Man discovered that no two people had identical fingerprint characteristics in the same position and number of ridges apart from each other. There are similarities, but no two different person's fingerprints are identical. A system was devised for recording, filing, and searching these different sets of fingerprints. The pattern and characteristics remain the same all through a person's life and never changes except for size and the texture of the skin.

"Even after death, the frictional ridge patterns remain the same until decomposition sets in and the skin falls off of the body. The fingerprint patterns are made up of ridges and furrows. Even after the finger heals from a temporary cut, the ridge pattern comes back the same as it was before the injury occurred.

"The ridges form certain types of ridge characteristics: dots, ridge endings, enclosures, bifurcations, trifurcations, etc. Basically, we've discovered how to duplicate fingerprint patterns with the help of a new elasticized material that we've discovered. Here's the beauty of it. We enlarge a fingerprint to ten times its original size. Using these thin plastic strips, we can duplicate the entire pattern, ridge by ridge, characteristic by characteristic onto these rubber gloves.

"Here's how it's done. We place thin strips of our special material onto the ridges in the enlarged photograph. We can connect and separate the ridges as need be. When we've constructed the pattern, we dip the entire photo into a special solution. The solution reduces the strips down to the normal fingerprint size. I should have first told you that we placed a very thin layer of our material over the photograph before we applied the strips. When the strips are reduced, we just fasten the reduced print to a rubber glove. Actually, we use rubber cement to fasten the constructed print to the glove.

"The distance of the furrows between the ridges varies a little, but it's close enough so that nobody notices that it's a forged fingerprint. These *Wanted* posters with the fingerprint patterns on them were taken from the bulletin boards at local post offices. We've made duplicate fingerprint sets of these twenty-five men first. Once we've ironed out a few little kinks, we'll be able to sell these gloves to every hood and potential criminal in town -- and at a fat profit if I should say so myself."

"Sounds very interesting," said Vance, anxious to hear more, "but have you actually used these gloves to commit any crimes?"

"Open up the safe," said Stripes.

The young chemist spun the dial quickly on an old safe door. He turned the handle and pulled open the heavy metal door. Stripes reached into the safe and removed two large cloth bags. He showed the contents to Vance.

"Look inside of these bags, Clicker. See all that dough? We've been hitting a lot of good spots in the last five months. Office buildings, motels, hotels, loan offices -- you name it and we've been there."

And I bet they even killed that night watchman, thought Vance. Wait until Captain Reese hears this bit of news.

Vance looked at his wrist watch, "Hey, it's getting late. I've got to be going. I've got a lot of things to do tonight."

Stripes threw the bags of money back into the safe and slammed the metal door shut. He turned the handle and spun the dial around several times.

"Where are you going that's so important?" asked one of the chemists.

"Probably has a hot foxey lady waiting for him -- hot and anxious," remarked the other chemist, laughing.

"Yea, you hit it right on the head guys, I haven't seen her in a couple of weeks and my loins are killing me."

"You stay with me tonight, we've got a lot more important things to do. Our task will take us most of the night. The foxey lady can wait."

Vance was stuck. He couldn't leave without arousing suspicion. "All right, Stripes, I can wait."

Stripes spoke to the two chemists. "Guy's," he began, "I have a small problem. My pill factory went up in smoke tonight. The boilers blew and sent the whole building flying in every direction."

"Is that where he got that cut and beautiful lump on the side of his head?" asked one of the chemists, pointing to Vance's head.

"Yea, he was there working when the place went up."

"What do you want us to do, Stripes?"

"It'll take me awhile to get more equipment, but in the meantime I'll be able to push the *LSD*. You'll have to whip me up another batch of the stuff so we can start shipping it out as soon as possible so I can fill my orders."

"Do you want us to stop working on the special fingerprint project?"

"For a few days anyway. That's all the time it should take to whip together another batch of drugs."

"Anything you say," answered the chemist. "You're the boss, Stripes."

"I've got an appointment at box sixteen tonight. I'm taking Clicker with me. If I finish there early enough, we may come back here and give you a hand."

"Box sixteen?" remarked Vance. "Just what in the hell is that?" Another one of your special codes, Stripes?"

Stripes smiled. "Never you mind what it is. We'll be there in half an hour. You'll see what it is then."

110

Vance and Stripes left the warehouse, got into the car and drove off. The trip was a short one. They drove along a dark, unpaved dirt road that took them deep into the railroad freight yards. Stripes finally stopped the car.

"This is as far as we can go by car," said Stripes. They both got out of the car. Stripes started walking as he spoke. "We'll have to hoof it on foot the rest of the way."

"Is it very far from here?" asked Vance. He chuckled. "Hey Stripes, are we gonna play Jesse James and stick up a train?"

"Never mind the corny jokes Clicker, just follow me. We'll be there in a couple of minutes."

The short jaunt took them through several roundhouses, a storage warehouse, and across several hundred feet of railroad tracks. They approached several wooden boxcars coupled together on a lone track at the extreme back portion of the railroad yards. Stopping at the last boxcar, Stripes knocked on the large wooden sliding door.

"Do you expect to find anybody at home?" laughed Vance.

Stripes gave Vance a look of annoyance, then knocked on the sliding door again.

"*Who is it?*" shouted a voice from inside of the boxcar.

"*It's me, Stripes! Open up!*"

A latch turned and the large wooden door slid over to one side. There was a grayish, blue haze inside of the boxcar. The air reeked with the sweet pungent odor of burning straw.

Another pot party, thought Vance. What a beautiful spot to have one. Just far enough away from the prying eyes of the law. The guard at the door helped to boost Stripes up into the boxcar. Vance pulled himself up.

Kerosene lanterns, hanging from the ceiling, illuminated the inside of the boxcar. Young kids lined the walls, inhaling the bluish smoke from their marijuana cigarettes. Stripes reached into his pocket and removed several foil packets. He handed them to the guard at the door.

"Where's Ortega tonight?" asked Stripes. "Is he here?"

"*Hey! Ortega!*" shouted the guard. "*Someone here to see you!*"

111

A figure, in the far darkened corner of the boxcar, pushed the girl off his lap and stood up. He pulled the zipper up on the front of his pants and walked towards Stripes. He smiled when he saw who it was.

"Hello Senor Stripes. How are you tonight?"

"Not too good, Ortega. I've had a run of bad luck all week long. Anyway, I brought the foil packets that you wanted."

Ortega's look at Vance was unusually strange. Stripes instantly caught the uneasiness that developed between both men.

"What's wrong, Ortega? Is something bugging you?"

"Yes, Senor Stripes, something is bugging me! Where did you pick up this guy?"

"This is Clicker, my partner. We've been together for about a year now. He's been helping me out with my drop-offs and pick-ups."

"I bet he has," replied Ortega. "When was the last time we met -- Senor Martall?"

Ortega's last statement completely took Vance by surprise

"That was the same name that Rea had mentioned," said Stripes. "Clicker, do you two know each other?"

Vance paused before speaking, then shook his head from side to side. "No!" he answered.

"Oh, this fellow knows me all right, Senor Stripes. Don't you, Senor Vance Martall?" Ortega sarcastically remarked. "That get-up you're wearing doesn't fool me. Senor Martall and I go way back to our days in the military service. Study my face carefully -- Senor Martall. I'm sure you'll remember me -- Rafael Ortega. I was a supply sergeant then. I had the sweetest deal working with the black market. Senor Martall here, was working as an undercover agent for Military Intelligence.

"Because of him, my nice little racket folded and I was sent to a federal penitentiary for three years. Oh yes, I know him very well. I swore that someday I would find him and have my revenge. I was successful in tracking him until about a year ago, that's when he graduated from the Police Academy. He just seemed to vanish into thin air. It was as if he never existed. I couldn't find out anything more about him. That only means one thing -- he's working undercover again!"

This was it for Vance. His cover was blown. His only chance was to make a break for the door.

112

Stripes turned and stared unbelievingly at Vance. His eyes showed that crazed look he had the night Rea was killed. Vance knew what was waiting for him if he didn't make a fast exit from the boxcar.

Stripes reached into his back pant's pocket and pulled out Rea's blue steel .38-caliber revolver. Pointing it at Vance, his hand shook unsteadily from the anger that overtook his reasoning powers.

"Hey, old buddy," laughed Vance, trying to catch Stripes off guard, "you don't believe this crazy Mexican hop head, do you? Since when did you go in for carrying those things?" he asked, pointing at the gun.

"*Shut up! Just shut the fuck up you dirty no good son-of-a-bitch!*" screamed Stripes. "*It was you all the time. I never had such a run of so much bad luck. My bad luck, was keeping you around me. It was because of you that Sorento and Monica died. You caused that slip up at City Hall on purpose. I killed Rea because of You! You blew up my house and all of my merchandise inside of it. All of the contacts that were caught after you made the deliveries, was because of you -- You bastard! You no good fuckin' bastard! You did this to me!*" He continued screaming at the top of his voice. "*Get out -- get out of here -- all of you! I'm going to take care of this guy myself.*"

The boxcar quickly emptied out. Within moments, Vance and Stripes were alone -- facing each other. Stripes slowly pulled back the hammer on the gun.

"You're gonna get it good, Clicker. I'm gonna really enjoy watching the pain in your face when I keep pulling this trigger, and those lead bullets keep ripping into your stomach. The only thing I'm gonna be sorry about is that -- *I Can Only Kill You Once!*" Lifting the gun up higher, Stripes remarked, "It's been fun Clicker, but your time has just ran out!"

Vance felt an unusual sensation at the bottom of his feet. Suddenly, the floor of the boxcar started vibrating. Stripes' deep concentration, on killing Vance, made him totally unaware of these vibrations.

BANG -- the boxcar jolted forward sending Vance and Stripes bouncing off the wall onto the floor. Stripes dropped the gun. As it hit the floor, it fired, sending a bullet flying wildly into the roof of the boxcar. Vance was the first one on his feet. There was no time to try for the gun. It was closer to Stripes. Vance made a mad dash for the door, jumped down onto the stone gravel bed, and started running.

Stripes picked up the gun, got up from the boxcar floor and ran to the doorway. He stopped and listened. The stillness of the night carried the sound of Vance's feet running on the crushed gravel.

"*I'll get you, Clicker. You can run,*" he shouted, "*but I'll get you --- you son-of-a-bitch!*"

Stripes jumped down from the boxcar, pursuing Vance through the railroad yard. He knew a short cut that would take him to the car first. Stripes figured that was where Vance was headed.

When Stripes reached the car, Vance wasn't there yet. He hid on the side of an old tanker car, waiting quietly and patiently for Vance to arrive.

The dark shadow of a man moved slowly through the railroad yard -- heading straight for Stripes.

That had to be Vance, thought Stripes. Who else would be wandering around the freight yards at this time of night? He felt the excitement of a hunter stalking his prey.

Vance crept around the corner of a deserted building, cautiously watching where he walked. Startled when Stripes stepped out from the shadows in front of him, Vance tried to run, but his feet were paralyzed. Stripes was the first to speak. "Hi Clicker," he said coyly. "Just freeze right where you're at." Vance didn't make a move.

"It's all over, Clicker -- all over for you," said Stripes, laughing and gloating at outsmarting Vance back to the car. He squeezed the trigger until the gun fired. The bullet struck Vance in his left shoulder, sending him spinning around in a complete circle.

The stillness of the night was suddenly aroused by the movement of trains and squeaking boxcar wheels. A series of three boxcars moved on the tracks, heading straight for Stripes. He stood on the tracks, ignoring everything else around him with only one thought on his mind -- killing Vance.

The huge coupling on the first boxcar completely encircled Stripes' chest and dragged him along the tracks, eventually joining them with another boxcar's coupling. The night air carried Stripes' horrifying screams as the metal jaws latched themselves together, crushing his chest. In a few short seconds, it was all over for Stripes. His disfigured body dangled over the connected couplings -- motionless.

Vance struggled to lift himself off the ground, picked up the gun, and walked over to Stripes' body. He felt Stripes' neck for a heart beat, but there was none. Vance wanted to feel some remorse or some kind of pity for Stripes -- but he felt nothing. In fact, he was glad that the world was rid of Stripes and the misery he had brought to others. No, he wasn't sorry for Stripes.

What next? thought Vance.

CHAPTER 22

Vance's assignment still wasn't completed. At the warehouse, the two chemists still had to be dealt with.

An aching, burning sensation in his shoulder brought Vance back to realization. He was shot and his shoulder hurt like hell. Blood slowly flowed from the open wound that the bullet had made. He removed his shirt, examining the wound. It appeared that he had only sustained a flesh wound. Removing a clean handkerchief from his pocket, he made a bandage and tied it around the wound.

Vance walked back to the car. Fumbling through his pockets for the car keys, he suddenly remembered that they were back with Stripes. He couldn't go back to get them. The very thought of seeing Stripes' mangled body again appalled him. Besides, he had to get back to the warehouse as quickly as possible.

He knew he'd need help when he got to the warehouse. Somehow, he had to reach Captain Reese -- and in a hurry. Sitting on the front seat of the car, he yanked two wires off the ignition switch and reconnected them to two other hot wires. Taking a metal coin from his pocket, he inserted it into the ignition switch. Crossing his fingers, he twisted the coin slowly. The car engine started, purring like a contented kitten. Vance drove off looking for an outside telephone booth.

Captain Reese's telephone rang twenty-five times before Vance finally gave up. There wasn't enough time to go to a local police station. He'd have to do a lot of explaining, and then they might not believe him because of the way he looked. Besides, he didn't have any proof as to who he really was. Vance had to take care of this problem by himself.

The pain in his injured arm increased. He saw a large neon sign flashing on the next corner spelling out the word -- *DRUGS*. Walking to the drug store, he went inside and purchased a bottle of peroxide, a ball point pen, some envelopes, and a pad of writing paper. His walking pace slowed down as he made his way back to where the car was parked.

Vance had to pass Captain Reese's apartment building on the way back to the warehouse. He quickly wrote a few lines on a piece of paper explaining where he was going and asked the Captain to get there as soon as possible. He inserted the note into an envelope, sealed it, and wrote the Captain's name on the front.

Unscrewing the metal cap off the peroxide bottle, he poured half of its' contents over the compress on his arm. The sudden shock from the stinging bite of the antiseptic almost made him pass out. Forcing himself to stay alert, Vance drove to Captain Reese's building.

The apartment building was silhouetted against the darkened sky. Vance stopped the car in front of the main entrance. Getting out, he looked up towards the tenth floor. No lights were visible in any of the Captain's apartment windows.

Vance picked up the envelope off the car seat and walked into the main lobby. The south wall of the lobby displayed the mail boxes for the entire building. He sought out the compartment with Captain Reese's name on it. Finding it, he pressed the signal button above the name plate several times. There was no response.

He's definitely not home, thought Vance. He forced the envelope into the small mail slot. Positive that the Captain would spot the envelope sticking out of the mail slot when he came home, Vance left the apartment building, got into his car and drove off, heading for the warehouse.

The hands on Vance's wrist watch showed 2:58 a.m., when he stopped the car in front of Stripes' warehouse. Shutting off the engine and headlights, he remained seated, surveying the entire area. No signs of life were visible. He got out of the car and closed the door quietly, forgetting Stripes' gun on the car seat.

The wind felt cool and pleasant as it whipped passed his sweat soaked face. Above him, a full moon brightly illuminated the entire area. He tried the entrance door to the warehouse -- it was locked. He went back to the car and removed a screwdriver from the glove compartment. Inserting the head of the screwdriver between the door and door jam, he forced the door open without making to much noise.

The warehouse portion of the building was deserted. It was hard to see in the dark without the help of a flashlight. Vance felt his way along the long rows of dusty boxes. He saw a dim light shining through the second floor office window. The light helped illuminate a small portion of the warehouse floor.

Vance tried to analyze a plan for the apprehension of the two young chemists. He decided on just playing it by ear as he went along. Cautiously walking up the stairs, he suddenly stopped. Something was different in the warehouse. Then he realized what it was. The metal drums under the stairs had been moved to the other side of the building. He continued up the stairs, stopping when he reached the office door. Forcing a smile, he opened the door and walked into the room.

"Hi guys," He blurted out loudly.

"Are you alone?" asked one of the chemists.

"Yea."

"Where's Stripes?"

"He had another appointment to take care of first. He said he'd drop by later." Vance acted unconcerned with their questions.

"Is that so -- Senor Martall?" spoke a voice from behind him.

Vance felt a sharp stabbing pain at the base of his spine. "Don't make a move Senor Martall," the voice ordered. "There is a very sharp knife resting on your spinal cord. If you should happen to move, I don't think it would be very pleasant for you. Now, slowly raise your hands above your head."

Vance did as he was told. A hand searched through his pockets, removing several items, placing them on the table.

"And now, Senor Martall, please turn around slowly, but keep your hands up in the air."

Vance obeyed.

"Where is Senor Stripes -- Senor Martall, or should I call you -- Officer Martall?" asked Rafael Ortega.

"What are you talking about Ortega?" asked one of the chemists.

117

"This very smart fellow, we have standing here in front of us, is really an undercover police officer."

"What are you going to do with him now that we've got him?" asked the other chemist.

"Don't you worry amigos, I have plans for our friend here. I have a personal score to settle with him. Bring your hands down and place them behind your back, Senor Martall."

Vance obeyed without hesitation. Ortega picked up a long length of electrical cord, he found on the floor, and tied Vance's hands behind his back. Vance screamed in pain.

"I see that you have injured your shoulder. That's too bad, you'll just have to endure all the pain and agony." Ortega pulled up a chair and forced Vance to sit down. He picked up Vance's personal belongings and shoved them into his own pant's pockets.

"Don't want to leave any evidence laying around, do we Officer Martall?" said Ortega laughing.

"Why don't you just give up Ortega? The police already know about this place. They'll be here at any moment. Make it easy on yourself."

"*Shut up!*" screamed Ortega, jumping up from his chair. He struck Vance across the face with the back of his hand. A tiny trickle of blood flowed from the corner of Vance's mouth.

"We've got to get out of here Ortega," pleaded one of the chemists.

"I told you two that I'd take care of everything." Ortega was losing his patience. On the other side of the long table, he opened a small drawer and removed a hypodermic syringe and needle.

"Have you chemists any of that chemical left from that batch you made up?"

One of the chemists handed Ortega a small glass vial filled with a clear liquid, covered with a rubber cap. Ortega inserted the needle into the vial through the rubber cap, and filled the syringe to capacity.

"What are you going to do with that?" asked one of the chemists, grabbing hold of Ortega's arm.

"Just watch me. You'll see." Ortega pulled his arm free from the youth's grasp. He headed straight for Vance.

"This'll keep you quiet until we're ready to leave. There's a small room down at the bottom of the stairs that's going to keep you on ice

118

for awhile. Shortly after I inject this drug into your arm, you'll be like putty in my hands." Ortega grabbed Vance's arm and jabbed the needle into the muscle. Vance yanked his arm away from Ortega's grasp, causing the needle point to break off. Only a small portion of the liquid entered his body.

"He's got enough in him to keep him quiet," said one of the chemists, "let's pack it up and get the hell out of here."

Ortega threw the syringe against the wall -- smashing it into tiny glass shards. He was angry he didn't have a chance to inject all the fluid into Vance's arm. Within minutes, the chemical started to take effect. Ortega lifted Vance from the chair, dragged him over to the doorway, opened the door, and dragged Vance over the threshold. He stopped at the top of the staircase.

"No sense in tiring ourselves out carrying him down these damn stairs," remarked Ortega. He gave Vance a push with his foot that sent him tumbling down the stairs -- head over heels.

When Vance bounced off the last step, Ortega walked down the stairs, grabbed Vance by his heels and dragged him into the small room. He propped Vance up against a wall and walked out of the room, bolting the door shut from the outside. Confident that Vance couldn't escape, Ortega went back to the office and helped the two chemists pack.

Several minutes passed. Vance began to slowly come back to consciousness. His mind was hazy, but not enough to keep him from realizing that he had to do something to get himself free. Applying all of his human strength, Vance managed to stand up straight. Every bone in his body ached. He looked at his shoulder. His wound had started bleeding again. Somehow he had to get his hands free.

Looking the room over, he discovered that he was in a bathroom. He knelt down and inserted his hands into the urinal bowl. The ice cold water enabled him to slide his hands free from his wire bonds. His hands had shrunk just enough from the cold water to let him perform this task.

Exerting all of his reserve strength, he tried to force the door open. He failed. He had to find another way of getting himself free. Vance peered through a small crack in the wall and saw that the warehouse lights had been left on. From what he could see, no one was in the lower part of the warehouse. Feeling his way around the room, he found a wooden crate in one corner of the bathroom. Using the crate as a foot stool, he succeeded in punching a hole in the decayed ceiling planks. He succeeded in making an opening approximately twelve inches by twelve inches.

How could he stall Ortega and the chemists until Captain Reese got there with the troops? he wondered. He found a full roll of toilet paper lying on the floor. An idea came to him. If it worked, it would keep Ortega and the two chemists busy -- at least till help got there.

Unraveling a portion of the paper roll, Vance stood on the wooden crate and prayed that his first shot would be a good one. There would be no second chance if he failed. Taking careful aim, he threw the roll of paper through the small opening in the ceiling. He felt like a basketball player shooting that last important shot at the hoop -- that would win the game. The roll of toilet paper flew through the air, unraveling itself as it went along, and landed inside one of the open cartons on the other side of the room.

BINGO, thought Vance, right on target. He fumbled through his pockets and found a crumpled book of matches that Ortega had overlooked. Vance suddenly felt dizzy and sick to his stomach. He stuck two of his fingers down his throat and vomited.

It took a little while, but he felt better. Continuing with his task, he tore the last match out of the booklet. He prayed as he lit the match and touched the bright red and yellow flame to the dangling piece of toilet paper. The flames swiftly crept up the length of paper, heading first for the ceiling and then out of the small opening.

Vance went back to the small crack in the wall and watched the length of paper get smaller and smaller as the flames quickly consumed it. The hungry flames finally reached the box of packaging materials. Within seconds, the hot flames jumped from one box to another, resembling a giant squid throwing forth its tentacles.

Vance had to get out of that warehouse -- fast. With every bit of energy that he had left, he managed to climb back on to the wooden crate. He tore away small chunks of wood from the ceiling to increase the size of the opening. Chinning himself upward, he carefully squeezed through the opening and boosted himself up onto a wooden beam, connected with the opposite wall of the warehouse. His shoulder ached terribly, as did his back and sides from the scratches he had sustained when he crawled through the hole in the ceiling.

He spotted a glass skylight in the warehouse ceiling, approximately fifty feet from where he was resting. Heavy, thick, black clouds of smoke quickly filled the entire warehouse. Vance's lungs burned unmercifully with each breath that he inhaled.

Suddenly, the door to the second floor office opened. Ortega and the two chemists ran out of the office, down the stairway carrying fire extinguishers to put out the spreading flames. Within minutes, they discovered that they were trapped by the flames.

Because of the age of the building, the hungry flames were running out of control. Vance slowly dragged himself along the wooden beam. The angry flames tried to consume his shoes and pants. The hair on his legs began to singe from the heat that was getting unbearable.

Vance finally reached the window. He smashed the glass with his elbow and pulled himself up through it. Frantically, he beat at the flames engulfing his pants, using only his bare hands. He could only extinguish some of the flames. The skin on his hands turned to raw flesh, burnt tissue, and blisters. The sharp gravel on the roof sheeting cut into his hands and knees as he crawled upwards towards the peak of the roof.

Reaching the roof's peak, he heard the wail of screaming sirens coming from the distance. He could see the tiny, flashing lights heading straight for the warehouse. He smiled weakly as he painfully dragged himself down the opposite side of the roof, knowing in a very short while he would be rescued.

Reaching the rain gutter, he fainted just as a tremendous explosion erupted from within the warehouse. Vance's body was thrown from the roof. He landed between a set of railroad tracks running along the side of the warehouse.

A loud blast from a horn brought him back to reality. To him the horn sounded like the ones used on the approaching fire engines. Vance lifted himself up from the ground and turned around, only to find out that it wasn't a fire engine approaching him, but a moving locomotive pulling twenty boxcars -- just ten feet away from him.

The entire roof had collapsed into the flaming inferno. It took the Fire Department several hours to extinguish the flames. Then, the task of searching for bodies began. Rummaging through the smoldering embers, the firemen were successful in locating some charred personal articles, and charred fragments of human remains under the piles of rubble.

Several of the metal fragments that were found were of particular interest to Captain Reese. They had survived the intense heat and explosion. The name, *Clicker,* was scratched into a knife blade, a small camera, and a cigarette lighter.

Vance had completed his assignment, thought Captain Reese.

CHAPTER   23

At 10:00 a.m., exactly one week to the day following the warehouse explosion, three men were having a discussion. Captain Reese was sitting in a chair opposite of Mayor Cotagney. He handed the Mayor a briefcase containing all the articles found at the fire, along with a brown manila portfolio. The Mayor opened the briefcase, placing everything on the table in front of him.

"Is this everything I'll need for the press conference this morning, Captain Reese?" asked the Mayor.

"A full statement with all the information that you'll need is inside of that portfolio, sir," answered Captain Reese.

Mayor Cotagney removed the prepared statement from the portfolio and read the first three paragraphs aloud:
> "A week ago, Officer Vance Martall, working as
> a special undercover agent for this city and the
> police department, sustained serious injuries in the
> performance of his duty. His help was vital in
> ending some of the drug traffic in this city."
> -- et cetera -- et cetera -- et cetera.

Mayor Cotagney stopped reading after he finished the third paragraph. He inserted the statement back into the portfolio and closed it. He looked at the man laying in the bed next to them.

"Well, Officer Martall, how does that sound to you?"

Vance smiled. "Well, at least that'll inform the public on what's been going on in this city," he commented. "I'll have to create a new identity for my next assignment, and speaking of assignments, just what is my next assignment, Mayor?"

"For now, just let those injuries heal. You know Officer Martall, it was very lucky for you that we found you when we did. Your wounds were severe and you needed a blood transfusion right away. Please tell us again just how you got away," asked the Mayor.

"When the explosion occurred, it blew me off the roof, throwing me to the ground. A loud blast from a horn made me come around to my senses. I stood up and turned around, just in time to see a train bearing down on me. I jumped to one side, with the train only missing me by inches. I jumped out of the way and fell again, hitting my head on a rail. I rolled into the large weeded area next to the railroad tracks and fainted. My body was hidden from view -- all except for one part -- my hand. It's lucky for me that a fireman saw my hand sticking out of the weeds when he was running by me."

"We have to leave you now, but we'll be in touch in a couple of days, " said the mayor. "The Captain and I have an important press conference to attend back at City Hall."

Both the captain and mayor stood up, shook hands with Vance, and said good-bye. They took the elevator down to the first floor and left the hospital building.

Ten months from the day of the warehouse explosion, Sergeant James Shaw stood in front of a class of recruits in their tenth week of training at the Chicago Police Academy.

"Good morning, recruits," he began. "Today you'll be studying a new subject that was introduced into our training program. We have a special guest with us who will be conducting these classes. I'll leave it up to him to tell you what the program consists of and what he expects you to get out of this class. Officer, would you please come up and take over this class," said Sergeant Shaw.

The officer standing at the back of the classroom, walked up to the front and faced the recruits. His neatly pressed uniform, shined shoes, and military styled haircut demanded respect for the position he held. He stood behind a wooden podium, holding the top of it with both hands. His right foot rested comfortably on the bottom wooden support brace.

"Good morning, recruits," he began. "My name is Sergeant Vance Martall. This class will deal with the problems of doing street undercover work. I'll begin this class with one statement -- *It's a living hell out there -- and don't think otherwise!"*

ORDER FORM

Mail To:
Terk Books & Publishers
P.O.Box 160
Palos Heights, IL 60463

Ship to:
Name _____
Title _____
Organization _____
Street Address _____
City _____ State _____Zip _____
Phone _____
(In case we have a question about your order)

Quantity	Title	Unit Price	Total
SUBTOTAL			
· TAX: Illinois residents add 8.75% sales tax --unless exempt.			
SHIPPING/HANDLING: $3.50 for first item, 50¢ each additional item			
TOTAL AMOUNT			

TERK BOOKS

DEATH DANCED AT THE BOULEVARD BALLROOM
by Thomas E. Krupowicz
ISBN: 1-881690-00-8 — $12.95

FINGERPRINTS — THE IDENTITY FACTORS
by Thomas E. Krupowicz
ISBN: 1-881690-01-6 — $39.95

FIRST LINE DEFENSE
by Thomas E. Krupowicz
ISBN: 1-881690-02-4 — $9.95

DEAD MEN DON'T DRINK VODKA
by Thomas E. Krupowicz
ISBN: 1-881690-03-2 — $14.95